MAGIC ON A DIME

Oh a Canadian Dime!

RODNEY CONWAY

LifeRich Publishing is a registered trademark of The Reader's Digest Association, Inc.

LifeRich Publishing books may be ordered through booksellers or by contacting:

LifeRich Publishing
1663 Liberty Drive
Bloomington, IN 47403
www.liferichpublishing.com
844-686-9607

ISBN: 978-1-4897-4622-1 (sc)
ISBN: 978-1-4897-4621-4 (hc)
ISBN: 978-1-4897-4706-8 (e)

Library of Congress Control Number: 2023906276

Print information available on the last page.

LifeRich Publishing rev. date: 03/31/2023

"Oh its a Canadian dime,
you know the one with the boat on it."

CONTENTS

CHAPTER 1

Cid was going crazy. At least he thought he was going crazy—although if you are really crazy, you don't know much about it. Just the same, he was sure that if he told anyone else, they would be convinced that he was crazy. After all, this couldn't really be happening. He just couldn't be seeing what he was really seeing, and that was the problem; it didn't make any sense. It didn't. He kept telling himself that. He couldn't explain why his face was stuck to the glass and he was staring through the window at something unreal.

To convince himself that he was not seeing what he was in fact seeing, he tried various things that he believed would get rid of it. First, he stood outside his front door and stared at what he was seeing. Then he went back to bed and undressed and got under the sheets. Then he got up, dressed, and looked out the window again. It was still there. He checked for drugs in his medicine cabinet—nothing. He searched the recyclable bag and read and reread the label on the Rhône wine he had drunk the night before. He looked for mold on his cheese. Nothing changed the picture. What he saw was still there.

He then looked out his kitchen window twice and poured himself another cup of coffee. What he saw was still there.

Why me? he thought. *I mean, I'm nuts, but I'm not nuts like this.* "I am eccentric!" he yelled. The problem just would not go away. He wasn't on drugs; he was confident of that. So what was the answer here?

He looked out the window at his little boat tethered to the dock. The *Little Bluenose* was his pride and joy. The only issue was he didn't know how to sail it. He didn't even know why he had bought it and cleaned it up. It was a little one-mast fishing boat that in Cid's mind became the *Bluenose*, the most famous sailing schooner in seafaring history. But he didn't know how to sail it. So it was docked. It had become a fit symbol of Cid's life and dreams. But now there was a problem that overshadowed even that dilemma.

Cid had to face this present dilemma and could not procrastinate any longer. He turned from the window and carefully put his coffee mug down by the sink. He steeled himself, and with his heart in his mouth and his stomach churning, he lurched out his front door and started walking toward the *Little Bluenose*.

"Look calm," he said to himself and held his head high and shoulders back. He decided that he would just march right up to his boat, look up, and face it. That was what he thought he was doing until he got to his boat and was looking down at the beach, unable to raise his head.

Someone cleared their throat. Cid realized that it wasn't him. He looked up, and there it was, in full daylight. There was a goblin on his boat.

Goblins, as anyone who has read anything on goblins knows, are green. The trouble is that no one has ever really seen a goblin before. Apparently, they have rather large ears, huge wolfish grins, and large feet; that is what goblins are expected to look like. And of course, they are green. This goblin fit all the requirements except the color one. It was gray. It also carried a big stick. It was a big stick that looked like a staff or a spear handle or something large to bonk someone with.

Cid stared at the goblin. The goblin smiled down at him. The goblin stood around four foot and a bit. The gray skin was puzzling, and the staff looked dangerous. At that point, Cid wished he smoked or had some kind of reassuring habit that he could fortify himself with. All he had was a mouth that fell open and eyes that seemed to forget how to blink.

"You're a—"

"Goblin." The goblin spoke and smiled a wolfish grin. "My name's Scar."

"You talk." Cid was stunned.

"So do you. You have any coffee up there?" Scar pointed toward Cid's little sandstone house.

Cid fainted.

Fainting might not have been a very smart thing to do in this circumstance. Then again, no one else had ever met a goblin, so Cid, at this point, could be forgiven. Anybody could have fainted.

Cid didn't have a history of fainting. He saw stars sometimes if he got up too fast, and he got woozy at the sight of blood, but he never fainted,. Aside from a ridiculous fear of heights, he could be said to be quite tough. He also didn't like going on Ferris wheels or driving too fast. He was no coward, however, and even if fainting wasn't a good idea, it did him no harm this time. Luckily, he didn't hit his head on a rock and only landed in the sand. The sand cushioned him.

When he woke up, he was in his house with a blanket covering him, and a smiling Scar was handing him a warm cup of coffee.

"You fainted."

"Yeah, I did. Uh—" Words were a bit confusing for Cid at this point.

"I had to carry you up here. I thought the couch would be the best spot to put you. I found the blanket in your bedroom."

Cid found that he could only stare at Scar. The grayness of Scar stood out against the living room's green walls.

Scar sat down on the reclining chair next to the couch Cid was collapsed on. "Look, I get it. You've never met a goblin before, and you don't know what to think. You can't figure out if I'm real, and you are wondering if you've gone crazy, right?"

Cid nodded and then took a sip of the coffee.

"Good coffee, isn't it?" Scar asked.

Cid nodded.

"Good. Now we need to talk."

And so they began talking, mostly about Cid and his life and his unfulfilled dreams. Scar seemed to relish the part about studying commedia dell'arte in California and attending acting school in New York and was puzzled by Cid's sputtering career.

"I've come close," Cid remarked. "But I've never reached my goals."

"Hmm, too bad." Scar sipped his coffee, shaking his head.

"This is weird," Cid announced. He put his coffee down. "Just weird."

"What? Talking with a goblin? Imagine how I feel—everyone thinks I'm imaginary. It could be worse, though. You could be here talking to Santa Claus."

Cid smiled but didn't tell Scar about the suit in his bedroom closet.

"So, Cid, what about that boat?"

The question caught Cid off guard. It made him uncomfortable; it was a subject that he didn't like to discuss. It was a dream that he had wanted to fulfill. He just thought he couldn't do it and had come to the conclusion that he had to face reality and get on with his life.

"It was an impulse, just an idea. I thought ... then I bought it and cleaned it up, and I just have all these ideas, but I just—"

"Have you ever sailed it?"

"No!"

"Have you ever sailed ever?"

Scar was sitting on Cid's reclining chair, his big goblin feet resting on the footrest. It was a bit odd to see a goblin sitting in Cid's favorite spot.

"Once, I went out on a sailboat on Lake St Clair."

"And?"

"I loved it. I mean, I got a bit seasick, and then I kind of got over it."

"So you went out on a sailboat once, but you have never sailed a boat yourself or even had someone show you how to sail?"

"Yes."

"Hmm."

"What?"

"Let's go sailing."

"When?"

"Now. Let's go out on your boat, and I'll teach you a few tricks of sailing."

With that, Scar jumped to his feet and headed out the door.

Cid sat for a moment in a bit of shocked disbelief, and then something occurred to him, and he ran out the door after Scar.

It took Scar a short time to get the boat launched as he barked out good-natured orders to Cid. Scar taught him *aft* and *stern* and *starboard* and *lee side* and as many nautical terms as made the task easier. He was easy about it and showed great patience repeating himself so that Cid could grasp what was being instructed.

They sailed out toward the horizon. For the first time ever, Cid could see what his home looked like from the sea. Throughout the day, he would look landward at his little house. It was odd and strangely beautiful. This was a hint of what he had been dreaming of. He had known that he had a bit of fear for the ocean but had wanted to challenge that fear. This was the beginning of facing that very challenge.

To view the ocean from land was one thing—to be on it was a whole greater dimension. At first, the tidal motion felt fine to him. When the boat hit the first swell, Cid had some second thoughts, but Scar kept him busy with the sails.

They spent the afternoon out in the bay sailing and tacking, and Scar put Cid through as many simple techniques as Cid could handle. Cid was excited; this was everything he had wanted to do with this little boat.

He could see in the distance the lighthouse near his home. He could just make out his little sandstone house and the dock out front. He thought of all the times he had stood on the dock and on the *Little Bluenose* and dreamed of actually sailing. Gratitude for what Scar had done welled up in him and brought a lump to his throat. Then he remembered something that he hadn't told Scar.

"I put the *Bluenose* up for sale."

"So?" Scar asked him.

"Well, someone is going to come and see it and possibly buy it."

"You are not going to sell it."

"I told him that I would."

"Tell him that you changed your mind."

"I can't."

"When?"

"In three days."

"We need to tack."

"Tack, right. What am I doing?"

"Haul that line, Cid. Duck. Watch out for the boom."

That was the last thing that Cid heard before the boom connected with his head.

Cid regained consciousness to find Scar's face inches above him, plastered with that crazy grin. Cid tried to look around. The sky was still blue, and they were floating up and down.

"Good you're still alive."

Scar moved away, and Cid's world went dark.

CHAPTER 2

CID WAS IN A HAZE, AND SOMEONE WAS CARRYING HIM INTO THE bright sunshine. He felt cocooned in blankets, and he remembered seeing his painting of trees beside his bed. Then a strange man was prodding his head gently and talking.

A light turned on in Cid's head. A shaman waving strange beads and chanting musically was dancing around his bed. *Where am I?* Cid thought. Perhaps the light was outside his head. He sat up to look at the light. The shaman kept dancing.

"Is this covered by my medical insurance?" The brief moment of clarity ended, and Cid then collapsed back into a fretful sleep.

People were talking in the next room, yet none of them was discernible, muffled voices and sounds. It seemed that they were moving back and forth outside the house. Everything was in a blur of waking and dreaming, a cacophony of events.

Cid heard Scar's voice and other voices. There was bright sunshine and dark, thick night.

Sleep took over.

A voice, a stranger's, said that Cid was fine now and he would sleep comfortably. "Let him rest," the stranger said.

CHAPTER 3

CID WAS IN A DREAM. IN HIS DREAM, HE WAS STANDING ON A SMALL hill overlooking an endless plain. Gray clouds filled the skies. There was no grass on this plain, just endless flat ground. He thought that it must be a dream. He turned in a circle, and everywhere was this endless monotonous plain. The plain was unpopulated, devoid of life, not even a blade of grass. Cid stood there transfixed, awed by the relentless boredom.

Suddenly, a dot appeared out of nowhere, and as it came closer, Cid saw that it was a person. Someone was walking toward him. As he approached, Cid saw that he was a warrior. He wore dark leathers and a round shield and carried a sword. For some reason, he looked familiar to Cid. He was tall like Cid and had shoulder-length brown hair. He looked young yet experienced. As he got closer to Cid, he started to converse.

"This plain is endless. A man could get lost forever on this plain."

"Yes, I suppose that he could," Cid answered.

"It is like an endless plain of Limbo."

Hearing *Limbo* terrified Cid. The word grated on his soul. It shook him to the core. It felt like a giant boulder pressing down on Cid. He soon was perspiring.

"Don't leave me on this plain, Cid. I need you, and so do the others."

"Others? What are you talking about?"

"Look." The warrior pointed, and there were hundreds, thousands of people walking across the plain toward Cid. Where had they come from? They were not all the same peoples either. They were of different nationalities, shapes, and sizes. There were warriors who looked like the first man and one who looked like an emperor on a throne being carried by slaves. There were armies marching in unison and groups of individuals thrown together. He thought he saw someone in a rumpled suit. *A detective,* he said to himself. They looked familiar to Cid, but he was unsure. There were faces in the crowd that seemed familiar.

The warrior in front spoke out. "We need names, Cid. You created us, and you need to give us names and tell our stories. You have us stuck in Limbo. Cid, free us."

What the hell was he talking about? Cid was baffled. *Why me?* he thought.

"Names!" the multitude shouted, and they started shouting it in unison. "Names, names! Save us from Limbo. Give us names."

The emperor screamed at him, "You created us, and then you abandoned us!" He pointed some kind of scepter at Cid.

"Write our stories. Give us our names." The warrior stood before Cid and glowered at him, arms crossed over his chest.

The multitude pressed closer and closer to Cid. The sky behind them became a confusion of giant paintings and sketches, and Cid screamed and searched for somewhere to escape, but everywhere he turned was the endless plain. The people were everywhere, crowding him, begging, pleading, shouting for names.

Cid screamed. Blackness.

CHAPTER 4

WAVES. TO SEE THEM CRASHING ON A SHORE IS ONE THING; TO hear them rhythmically pounding the surf is another. At those moments, you are still somewhat detached, listening and viewing. To ride on top of ocean waves is a total sensation, inescapable in its effects. The sensation is overwhelming when unexpected. To be honest, even when expected, it can wash over you and grip all your sensations.

Cid woke up.

He thought that he was awake. He had this feeling that his world was floating and that he was rising and falling rhythmically. It pervaded his thoughts. He was in his room, yet he wasn't sure. He opened his eyes and tried to focus on something, anything. Everything was blurry, so he tried to focus on his window. The window seemed smaller than it should be. It also seemed round like a porthole. His world was swaying.

Suddenly, it dawned on Cid. *I'm on a boat; I'm on my boat, the* Little Bluenose. Thoughts of Scar scurried through his mind. He felt betrayed and hurt. *He stole my boat with me on it. God, I've been kidnapped ... by a goblin.*

All that Cid could think of was getting on deck and confronting Scar. The bed was a tiny alcove, and as he sat up, he hit his head on the top of the alcove. He carefully swung his legs out of the little cubbyhole and tried to sit up. The waves rocking the boat seemed to have other plans for him. His first attempt at standing only left him sprawled on the deck. He scrambled back up on the bed and grabbed some of his clothes out of a chest and struggled into them. His next try at standing was half-successful, and at least he reached the door and after several attempts pulled it open. Scar was his goal, and he was determined to get to him.

The immediate problem was those damn waves kept tossing the boat. The tossing seemed to be getting more extreme, and it was becoming difficult to decipher what was up and what was down. Cid somehow managed to both climb the ladder and crawl up it to reach the deck cabin above. As he glanced around, he did not see Scar in the cabin, but he caught sight of him out on deck manning the helm.

Scar was wearing a sou'wester and a huge slicker. Seeing Scar dressed like that made Cid realize he, too, had to cover himself. He kept proper storm clothing in a locker by the door that led out of the deck cabin. It wasn't easy, but Cid put the gear on. Luckily, he put on a harness, for as he stepped out of the deck cabin, he was flung to the starboard side of the ship. He briefly saw Scar at the wheel as he hurtled past. Scar, in good form, tried to grab Cid but missed, as he was still handling the wheel. Arms and legs waving in all directions, Cid smacked into the rail and wrapped his arms around it as best he could. As he was wrapping himself, he realized that Scar had set up a security line, so Cid hitched his harness to it. Now he could breathe.

What the hell am I doing out here? he yelled to himself. He looked at Scar and shook his head angrily. Scar, still grinning his big goblin grin, waved at Cid while still managing to keep his concentration on the sea. Where was he steering them? Cid was terrified and angry at being terrified and really annoyed at being kidnapped. In his head, the feelings just sort of convulsed. The sea was doing the same convulsive thing to Cid. All these things crashed into one another.

Every time Cid looked up, he saw massive waves coming down on the boat, and whenever he looked down, he felt like he was looking up. Holding on for dear life seemed to not be saving him from instant punishment and only magnify his discomfort. He decided that he would try to crawl to where Scar was and confront him. Unfortunately, Cid's timing was off, and he skidded sideways in any direction he was sent and therefore had quite a hard time reaching Scar.

After several crab-like attempts, he finally found himself close enough to yell and be heard. "Why did you ... ?"

"What?"

"You kidnapped me." Cid grabbed the mast to secure himself.

"You look like a goblin."

"What?" Cid shrieked as he began losing his grip on the mast.

"Look." Scar pointed at Cid's hands. "You're all green." Then he smiled and went back to concentrating on the helm.

Cid looked at his hand. As he was doing that, he was washed back toward the rail. He desperately clung on and spent the next several hours losing everything that ever wanted to remain in his stomach. All in all, the experience was awful, and thankfully, the sea did a good job of cleaning up any mess. Eventually, Cid slept, in between bouts of you know what and drenching from the waves. The harness kept him from being washed overboard. At various stages of his unpleasantness, Cid thought that drowning would be a pleasant alternative.

The night passed, and the next dawn revealed calmer seas. He had survived somehow.

"Two days," Scar told him.

"Which two days? What two days? What are you talking about? Is it an estimate or an announcement?" Cid curled up and refused to look at Scar.

"You've been sick for two days and nights." He sat down beside Cid on the deck and offered him a mug of coffee. "Drink this. It'll be good for you."

"What is it?"

"It's coffee!"

Cid took the mug and sipped from it. "You kidnapped me," he accused Scar and kind of sneered at him.

"Well, I couldn't sit down and debate the issue with you because you were unconscious. So, I did what was best for both of us and put you on board and set off."

This ticked Cid off. "Come on, you kidnapped me; you had no right."

"I need you and I need your boat." Beside Cid, Scar stretched his legs out on the deck and wiggled his feet.

"You need my boat? Damn." Cid sipped from his mug. "This coffee is good."

Yes. I need your help."

"Why kidnap me? That's a crime, you know."

Scar smiled and looked at Cid. "Sometimes, you have to break the law. Really, Cid, who would believe you if you reported this?"

Cid felt indignant. "The authorities."

"What authorities? What policeman or lawyer or judge would believe that you were kidnapped by a goblin?"

Cid didn't say anything. He just scowled.

"I thought so. See, even you don't believe it."

Cid just stared into his coffee mug. After a while, he let out a big sigh. Then he looked at Scar, who seemed to be just relaxing, soaking up the sun.

"Why do you need my help?"

"I have some friends who need to be saved," Scar said. "They have been out here on the ocean for a long time, and I need to find them. You were my last hope."

"Me?"

"Yes, you. You have destiny written all over you, Cid, and when I saw you and your boat, I knew that you were my answer."

"You were watching me?"

"For some time, I kept an eye on you. I had to be sure. Now I am sure." He toyed with his coffee mug and then looked at Cid. "I'm searching for some very dear friends that have been lost for a long time. I think that I know where they are and the only way to get to them is by sea."

"OK."

"I mean, no one else would even believe or stand for a goblin."

"I said OK."

Scar looked at Cid. Cid felt like Scar was staring into his soul. Scar held his gaze for a while and then offered Cid his hand. They shook.

"For now, I will be the captain, and I will teach you the basics of sailing and navigation. I brought some charts with me, and I'll show you how to read them and where I think that my friends are. This will be a great adventure, Cid. I appreciate what you are doing for me, and you will be rewarded." With that, Scar jumped to his feet and shouted, "Come on, let's get started!"

"Where?" Cid asked as he untangled himself from the rail. He followed Scar into the deck cabin. Scar had some charts spread out, and on one, he pointed to an island.

"I think there is where they are."

"I have no idea what I am looking at, so OK."

"It's far, very far. I think that we will need a bigger crew." As Scar said that, he walked out of the cabin and onto the deck. He gazed up at the sail and the one mast. "We have to transform this ship."

"I don't know what you are talking about."

"Sure, you do. It's an old acting exercise. You're an actor; you know how to do this." With that, Scar put his hands on his hips and stared at Cid.

"What are you talking about?"

"Theater magic."

"What?" Cid shook his head, stunned. "This isn't a play or a theater."

A strange look had come over Scar, almost a bewildered look. "Cid, the world is theater. Life is magic. When you are onstage, you transform your world. People believe you because they see it in your eyes."

"I know, but—"

"Trust me. Now, what do you see here?"

"I see the *Little Bluenose*."

"Good, but what was in your heart when you first set eyes on her?"

"I saw the *Bluenose*, the greatest schooner that ever sailed, the fastest ship alive."

"Good. Now hold that image, and let's go about transforming our dear friend into who she at heart really is."

With that, Cid gazed around at the *Little Bluenose*. He saw every line of his little boat from the mast to the deck. He knew this boat because he had stood on her and refurbished her lovingly for over a year.

As he was watching her, something happened. It started gradually, and then the ship changed. The change astounded Cid. Maybe the actor in him took over and he simply went with the magic, but it actually happened. The *Little Bluenose* was gone, and he now stood on the deck of the actual *Bluenose*. Cid's mouth hung open.

"Now we need a crew."

"A crew?"

"Yes."

"Where will you find a crew?"

"Don't worry. They're out there in boats waiting for us."

Cid sat down on the deck, his mouth hanging open.

CHAPTER 5

ANGUS MCFEE. THE NAME WAS LEGENDARY. CAPTAIN OF THE *Bluenose*. Most people remembered the ship but had forgotten his name. That was a tragedy to Dan; he wished it wasn't so. He had read everything about the *Bluenose* and loved its history. He would have loved to have lived in that time and sailed with Angus. He dreamed of hauling fish in off the Grand Banks and racing against wealthy Americans, beating them every time. Angus, it was said, ran a tight ship. Sailing with him and learning from the best would have been worth it. To Dan, Angus was the greatest sailor of all time.

Unfortunately, the heyday of schooners was long gone. Men weren't even fishing out of Lunenburg anymore. Not enough cod, they were told. The original *Bluenose* sank decades ago in a storm somewhere in the West Indies while hauling cargo, her glory days gone. Now there was the *Bluenose Two*—a replica, built exactly like its namesake but doomed to a life of stillness as a museum piece sitting in a harbor. This child, lovingly created, had been recently overhauled and restored once again. Its present life sometimes brought Dan, who loved its history, to sadness.

Dan, who would rather be out fishing, racing the seas on a swift schooner, was also stuck in the harbor—no fishing, no work unless he went west and hauled oil. That was why he was here working as a night watchman, watching over the *Bluenose*.

Generally, Dan sat in his watchhouse and on the hour wandered onto the boat and made his rounds. Tonight had been the same usual routine, nothing out of the ordinary.

At half past five in the morning, he detected a faint glow emanating from somewhere near the boat and jotted that in his logbook. He then proceeded to grab his flashlight and cautiously walked onto the boat. The glow was all around the *Bluenose*. It even appeared on him; he could see it on his hands and legs.

This is weird.

Dan went belowdecks to inspect further. Below deck were crates, unopened and seemingly newly delivered. They must have been put there during the daylight shift. He hadn't seen them yesterday evening. He continued his search and noticed more provisions. It all seemed odd.

He heard a noise from above and went to investigate. As he started to climb, he opened the hatch. Then the ship lunged, and Dan fell backward. Somehow, he landed on some coiled ropes, and feeling slightly woozy, he opened a door and fainted into a storage locker.

At seven o'clock that morning, the manager of the *Bluenose* Maritime Museum drove up to the parking lot, parked his car, and gazed over at the *Bluenose*. His head hit the steering wheel as he screamed and his horn blared out, disrupting the morning peacefulness. Instead of the *Bluenose Two*, there he saw a small one-mast fishing boat with the name *Little Bluenose* hand-painted on its stern.

CHAPTER 6

DAYS SPENT ADRIFT IN A LIFEBOAT SEEMED TO DRAG ON IN ENDLESS wonder. Thoughts became clouds, and clouds floated on endless skies. This time was like being in Limbo, endless, floating on eternal water. Fog seemed to be a constant, only interrupted by sun and dark. It was a dream state.

The trip hadn't been like this at first. The convoy had set sail from Halifax in the dark of night. Storms had dogged them for four days. A blessing, most of them thought, because the wolfpacks couldn't pursue them as easy. Then it had calmed down, and clear skies and seas had greeted them on the fifth morning. Sharp eyes were required, and nerves were on edge, constantly scanning the water.

Their little destroyer had tried to herd the ships it guarded, desperate to have them keep up. Then on the fifth evening, an explosion had gone up, and one slow liner had gone down.

The sonar had missed it. Lookouts had spotted nothing. Captain Fitch had ordered them to race back and hurry the other ships along.

Night had then descended, and while sipping coffee at his post, Stefan had seen a periscope and yelled and pointed. That was when the torpedo had struck amidships, and an explosion had thrown him to the deck. It was madness after that. All he could figure out was that by some miracle, he had ended up on this life raft.

Those remaining kept telling one another that they would be saved. They had some provisions, water and food. At first, there had been eight of them, but now, there were only five. They had been out here for so long that Stefan had to remind himself who he was. He was Stefan

Wilkes, petty officer first class of the Royal Canadian Navy. The others with him were the Chaplain Lieutenant Ross George, Chappy to the hands; Mr. Tubbs, master seaman (Stefan only knew him as Tubbs); Tom Smiley (Smiley as they called him), leading seaman; and Fred Rounder, master seaman and machinist. The others who had been with them had died within the first few days, so he had their names written in a little book tucked into his satchel. Periodically, Stefan would glance through the book and try to remember their faces.

The chaplain had saved those who remained by giving them hope, keeping their spirits up when all else failed, and then Smiley, of course, would laugh in the face of any dire emergency. Too bad he was out here; he would have made a great audience to some starving theater group.

Time, however, had gone wrong. It had lost all dimension, and the few men seemed to be floating endlessly. Time had become shapeless like the fog, and they just drifted in it. Sleep and wake had also become intertwined, drifting in and out endlessly.

The endless night had drifted into endless day and then a gray fog-like shroud. The war had abandoned them when the convoy had sailed on. The fear of U-boats had abandoned them also. They were alone in the stillness of damp fog.

Stefan felt a breeze on his face. It was a brisk breeze that made him wake up. He looked at his hand, and his compass was still sitting in it. His other hand was dangling over the side of the boat, and water was splashing over it. He looked at the others; they were all asleep still. Chappy was at the head of the raft clutching his Bible, muttering what sounded like prayers. Tubbs was snoring, his face relaxed. Smiley was slowly stirring, and Fred was curled up, sound asleep.

Stefan looked past Chappy. He'd begun calling the chaplain Chappy a few days after being in the raft. The chaplain didn't mind. He liked it, he said. As Stefan was looking at him, the fog that enveloped them cleared a bit. Stefan saw movement; it was a sailboat. The fog closed in again.

"A ship." Stefan tried to yell, but his voice only croaked it out.

It was enough, however, because Chappy's eyes opened wide, and Tubbs sat up and said, "Where?"

Stefan pointed, and all of them were sitting up by now. Chappy picked up the last water container they had and passed it around. They all stared into the fog where Stefan had pointed.

The fog suddenly lifted, and there on the horizon, sailing toward them, was the *Bluenose.*

"It's the *Bluenose.*" Stefan didn't sound sure of himself, but it looked like the *Bluenose.* He had once seen it with his father. "How can that be?"

Smiley looked at him. "I don't care if it's the *Queen Mary* or even a tugboat. It's seen us and it's coming to save us."

CHAPTER 7

CID WAS UNSURE OF HIMSELF AND THE DECK HE WAS WALKING ON. He knew that he just had to trust what was going on. That was easily said but a bit daunting in reality. Yet the ship was real. He could feel it. It had transformed from his little fishing boat into the actual *Bluenose.* It was a beautiful ship, incredibly elegant. It looked and felt real, so he kept telling himself that it was. Another part of him, the part he found himself sliding toward, said, "Wow, this is cool!" So, he stood on the deck and smiled.

Scar called to him. "Take the helm. I'm going below for a minute."

Cid came over and took the wheel.

"Just keep her steady on that heading."

"Is that fog up ahead?"

"It is, but I'm trusting it will lift."

Scar then left Cid to it and went below.

Dan found himself in a closet. It was one of the closets built into a ship to house safety gear and other necessities. This one seemed to contain rope and life jackets and other things. How he had toppled into this he couldn't quite figure out. He was annoyed at himself and dreaded the upcoming embarrassment when the day staff found him.

He thought the ship felt like she was underway, for some reason. *Why is the ship moving? How long have I been in here?* He glanced at his watch but could see nothing because it was too dark. He had to get out of this closet.

Behind him, he heard a noise and then a grunt, and then suddenly, light was everywhere.

"What are you doing here?"

Relief and embarrassment shot through Dan as he turned himself around and came face-to-face with a goblin.

"A goblin?"

"You are a stowaway."

"I'm not a stowaway."

"Yes, you are. And yes, I am."

"*You* can't be, and I am not."

"You're on our ship."

"You've stolen the *Bluenose*."

"No, we didn't."

"Then where am I?"

"You're five days out of Scotland heading roughly toward Newfoundland."

"What? Five minutes ago, I was in Lunenburg, Nova Scotia."

"What time?"

"Five o'clock in the morning."

"That makes sense. It's eleven in the morning here, at least by British time. I haven't adjusted my watch yet, and their time is six hours ahead of your time. We'll have to adjust our watches, it seems, as we travel along." Scar showed Dan his watch.

"But how did we get here?"

Scar shrugged his shoulders. "That must be the way the magic works, I guess." With that, Scar turned and headed back up on deck.

"Magic?" Dan puzzled over that statement, finding it hard to fathom.

"Come on up," Scar called back to him.

So, Dan followed the goblin, Scar, who shouldn't have been here really, up on deck of the *Bluenose Two*, which also shouldn't have been here.

"Hey, Cid, we have a guest."

Cid, at the wheel, looked surprised. "Who are you?"

"I'm Dan the night watchman. Who are you?"

"I'm Cid, and this is Scar."

Dan stood on deck and stared. They were at sea, all right, somewhere out on the Atlantic miles from anywhere. "You've stolen the *Bluenose Two*."

While saying that, something came over Dan, and he had to grin. He was at sea and aboard the *Bluenose*. The ship was doing what she was born for.

"Actually, we haven't stolen her. It's magic is all that I can tell you. We've done a borrowing or, in fact, an exchange, temporarily for now." Cid had a bit of a puzzled look on his face as he tried to explain it. "It's real—I mean, the ship is real. The fact that it's real takes a bit of trusting."

"It's real, all right. This ship was hand built with help from some of the men who actually built the original. She was newly restored just a few months back. This is a very real ship, and she is quite seaworthy." Dan was proud of *Bluey*, as he liked to call her.

"That's good. I wonder if my little guy is back at Lunenburg Harbor, then."

Scar scratched his neck and pondered that. "Could be. I never tried it on a ship before."

"What are you talking about?" Dan asked.

"Magic!" both Cid and Scar replied.

Dan ignored their answer, as something had caught his attention. "There's something out there. Look." He pointed toward where the fog seemed to be lifting. Both Cid and Scar strained to see where he was pointing. "There, it's a life raft, low in the water."

"I see it!" Scar yelled. "Cid, keep the helm steady. Steer toward them. Dan, since you know this boat so well, can you get us some gear, blankets, et cetera, anything we need to help starving, wet, cold sailors?"

"Aye, aye, Captain." Dan ran back down into the hold.

"Good lad, that one." Scar smiled. "Now let's save this lot. These men are precious, Cid. We need them as much as they need us."

"Are they who we are seeking?"

"No, but in another way, yes, they are part of this journey."

"How do you know that they are men?"

"Instinct and 40/20 vision."

Cid just stared at Scar. There was nothing he could reply with, so he shook his head and kept his hands on the wheel.

"I think that they have seen us. We'll try to edge right up to them. I'll throw a rope to them, and then I'll help them up."

"Scar, you should take the wheel and let me get them on board. Dan can help me. You might give them a fright."

"Oh right, I forgot that I am a goblin." Scar shrugged his shoulders and took the helm.

Dan came on deck carrying a stack of blankets. "I'll help get them on board, and then I'll make some hot tea to warm them up. I've got a first aid kit under the blankets just in case. I brought some water up also."

Scar maneuvered the boat to within a few yards of the life raft. Upon seeing the raft, Dan and Cid looked at each other with puzzled looks on their faces.

"How could this be?" Dan didn't know what to think.

Cid could only shrug his shoulders. "I don't know. I can't explain it, but I can tell that they need help."

"Yeah, but they're dressed like World War II sailors!"

"They still need our help."

"Yes, OK, let's get on with it," Dan said. "Hello down there! Grab this rope."

At the front of the raft, a middle-aged man who looked like a chaplain grabbed the rope as the others helped him. They got the raft alongside the *Bluenose*, and Dan climbed over to help them up. It took awhile with Dan pushing and Cid tugging, but eventually, everyone was on board. Somehow, Dan managed to tie the raft to the side of the boat.

Safely on board, the sailors all received blankets, and soon, hot tea and biscuits. None of them noticed Scar yet. The moment was fast approaching.

Stefan sipped his tea. "Oh, I dreamed of tea."

Tubbs retorted, "I dreamed of scones and Devon cream."

"Our prayers were answered. You saved us, you know. We'd been out there for ages." Chappy sighed and dropped his head to his chest. "I'd almost given up."

"Never, not you, Chappy. Old Fred Rounder would have perished without you, and so would have the others." Fred pointed at himself while speaking.

The others all chipped in, adding their approval and disagreeing with Chappy.

"You kept our spirits up, Chappy. I am not called Smiley for frownin', and you kept me smiling at the worst of times, old friend."

"You did your part, Smiley. We did it together. I want to say thanks to you folks for saving us."

Stefan looked up and started to ask Cid, "How did you get the *Blue*— Jeepers!" Behind Cid, Stefan could see Scar attending to the wheel.

Cid looked at him with sort of a smile on his face. "That's Scar. He saved your lives. He's a bit different than all of us, but I can vouch for him. He's not dangerous, and he's the best sailor I know."

"Is he from … ? I can't even guess," Tubbs snarled.

"No," Cid replied.

Chappy looked at Dan. "What have you to say?"

"Nothing. I've only been aboard for less than an hour. I was as shocked as you are."

Smiley started to stand up.

"Hold on!" Scar shouted.

Fred dropped his tea. "God, it speaks."

"Dan, take the wheel. Please just come over here. Keep us heading due west."

Dan rushed over to the wheel and took over. He was relieved; this, after all, was all that he had ever dreamed of, helming the *Bluenose Two* out on the open sea.

Scar walked over to the huddled group and stood looking down at all of them, which wasn't very far, because he wasn't very tall. "Now lookee here. We saved your lives, us three here. We took it upon ourselves to help you. Ignore the thought that I might look strange to you, being a goblin and all and just be grateful for our assistance. You owe us that much."

Stefan spoke up. "But you're a goblin."

Scar looked back at him. "So?"

"Goblins don't exist!" That was Smiley chiming in.

Scar looked at him. "I like you, probably because you seem to smile a lot. What's your name?"

"I'm Smiley."

"Good choice. I like you even more now. My name is Scar. How I got that name is a long story that I don't wish to repeat right now. We just saved your skins from what I bet was an awful long, listless time floating on the ocean. Am I right?"

The sailors all murmured in agreement.

"Right. Now, you are safe and dry, and after some sleep, we are going to fix you up with a decent meal. I don't want you to eat too much right now, because I bet you haven't eaten very much for some time. Cid will give you some broth and biscuits. Take it slowly, drink plenty of water. Then I want you all to rest and sleep. Tonight, we'll eat a meal, and I'll tell you what you need to know. I am a goblin, and it seems strange to you and unbelievable. I'm sorry about that. It will all make sense soon. Trust me; that's all I can ask."

The five sailors all looked at one another, and then Tubbs just shrugged his shoulders and Smiley laughed.

"I'd take you over a Nazi any day," Smiley chuckled.

With that, they all relaxed, Scar shook all their hands, and the five of them took some broth, which Cid dished out. After eating, they all simply fell asleep where they were, covered in blankets.

"How did you do that?" Cid asked Scar.

"What?"

"Get them to go to sleep on cue?"

"I didn't do anything. They're all really tired, and I bet they've been worrying themselves sick. This will be a non-stressful sleep for them."

So, Cid and Scar left them to sleep. They were soon joined by Dan.

"We still don't have enough crew," Dan said. Scar and Cid looked at Dan. "The original *Bluenose* had a crew of twenty-two. We only have eight people on board."

Scar gazed at the horizon. "Fog's coming back."

"Fog?" Cid replied.

"Fog comes, and fishing boats have to call in their crews. They ring their ships' bells, don't they, Dan?"

Dan looked at Scar with a puzzled look on his face. "Yes, they do, or did."

"It will do in this instance. We are crossing over time barriers here, guys. There were a lot of sailor fishermen lost in the fog out here. Let's help bring them home, shall we?" Scar walked over to the ship's bell and started ringing it.

The fog rolled in, and eeriness seemed to settle in with it. The peal of the bell reverberated off the fog.

"Ahoy there," a voice called out. It was from somewhere aft. Then another voice called out from off the port side.

Scar reached for a speaking tube and called out. "Follow the bell, and welcome aboard." Voices were calling out from all around the schooner. Cid counted at least nine dories all carrying fishermen.

"Well, there's our crew. We'd better help them on board."

All told, fourteen fishermen were welcomed on board. All of them had been adrift for some time, they reckoned—seven dories, all adrift on the Grand Banks, lost from their mother ships.

Cid met each dory, and as the men came on board, he welcomed them and explained as best he could that the ship was the *Bluenose Two* and the captain was a goblin. It was awkward to explain, so he just said it matter-of-factly.

The first pair were from a schooner out of Halifax. They were twin brothers. When they came on board, the first one, Bill, looked at Scar and said he looked like a gobley beast. His brother, Stan, laughed and said he still looked better than old Gisbon, the skipper of the *Sharkey*. They set right to work unloading the fish on their dory and started to toss them into the hold.

"This is a fishin' boat, ain't it?" Stan announced. "Some of you might as well help us with the catch."

Dan piped in. "I'll go below and start saltin' and preppin' them."

After that, as each dory came in, the fishermen set to work hauling in the catch. Half the men were below prepping the fish for storage. Even the sailors woke up and joined in the work. Dan had only read about this and seen this done in newsreels, but he took to it like a true salt. Cid was amazed as he watched it all and equally threw himself into the work.

Once everything was cleaned up, Scar announced that he would prepare a great feast and asked if anyone would like to help him prepare it. Chappy and Smiley both volunteered. "We'll drop anchor and sit for a spell," announced Scar, "and then we'll eat, and after, we'll talk."

Scar set to work and devised the most sumptuous pasta meal he could think of.

The rest of the day was spent welcoming sailors; explaining like mad the present circumstances; and, of course, finding places for each and every one of them to bunk.

Later, at sundown, Scar rang the ship's bell, and all the men met in the galley and sat down to eat. Everyone had a place to sit. Cid sat near Scar but tried to keep a low profile and endeavored to let Scar be the master of ceremonies. Dan helped Scar serve the food, and Cid set to pouring wine. The food was wonderful, a sumptuous, Italian feast. Lots of pasta, meatballs, antipasto, and laughter, and wine flowed throughout the meal.

One of the newcomers—a tall, lanky guy with wild reddish hair and a pronounced nose—piped up at the meal's start. "Mighty grateful to all of you. Never knew goblins could cook so good."

Scar smiled. "My mom taught me. Thank you. You're Reggie? Welcome aboard. Welcome all of you."

The men relished the food. And Scar had provided some decent Chianti to wash it all down.

Scar stood up and looked over all the men. "Best if I stand on my chair. It's a height thing." That brought some laughter. "Now, what I have to say is going to sound strange to all of you, although having a spaghetti dinner cooked by a goblin is in itself pretty strange, except if you are a goblin. Here goes. Cid and I have rescued you and have every intention of returning you safely to port."

Chappy stood and raised his glass. "For that, we thank you."

"Here, here!" they all shouted.

Scar bowed in acknowledgment. "However, we are on a mission, and we need your help in accomplishing this mission." He paused and looked at each and every one of the newcomers.

"There is a ship at sea that we have to find. This ship is called the *Forlorn Hope*. On it are some very dear friends of mine, and we are their only chance at salvation. These friends were unjustly punished many years ago. They, in fact, were condemned. They are my friends; they are family to me. I have a rough idea of where they might be, and I am intent on searching that part of the ocean. It may take some time. I am determined to find them. So, I am asking you all for your help."

"What about the war?" Stefan showed his worry, wringing his hands.

Most of the men seemed shocked. Stan, one of the brothers, asked simply, "What war?"

Scar held their attention. "Some of you might be alarmed. I don't blame you if you are. You are safe here. The war can't touch you."

Stefan showed his pain. "How can you say that? We were torpedoed."

No one else spoke. They all just stared at Scar. Then Smiley stood up and held up his wineglass.

"Are ya bein' straight with us, Mr. Scar?" Tubbs piped in.

"Very."

"How long will it take?"

"I'm not sure. Could be a couple of months, could be longer."

"What about the war that is raging?" Stefan was exasperated.

"Well, you see, that's another thing. What time do each of you think it is?"

Smiley looked at his watch. "Nineteen hours twenty-three minutes."

"What year?" Scar asked.

"1942."

With that, several others leaped to their feet and spoke.

"1925."

"1897."

"1933."

"2019," Dan said. He looked shocked but not as shocked as the others in the room. "It was 2019 when I walked onto the boat this morning. That was twelve hours ago."

Scar cleared his throat. "Gentlemen, this is going to be hard to believe, but right now, we are outside time. You all come from different times. While we are on this voyage, we will be sailing between times. When we are done, I will return you to your time and to a safe place. You will have to trust me on this. I will not let you down."

The men all looked stunned. There was much scratching of hands, and nobody spoke. The silence lasted awhile.

Smiley was still standing. He raised his glass again. "It seems a few hours ago, I thought that I was drifting off into Limbo. I believed myself dying. Now I am standing on a ship, drinking a terrific wine with fellow sailors. Mr. Scar, if you need my help, you've got it. Cheers to Mr. Scar!"

With that, the others stood up and gave their assent.

"OK, now that we are all agreed, why don't each of us tell everyone who we are and where we come from?" Scar suggested. "First, please trust me when I say that I am going to get you all back home. Let's start with you, Cid."

Cid was caught off guard. Just the same, he stood and looked around at the group. "I'm Cid. I am from Canada, but I live now on an island off of Scotland called Islay. They make great whiskey there, by the way. I live in a little sandstone house, and I am trying to be a writer, but it's been a slow process. I trained to be an actor, but that life is tough to get work in. I'm here because Scar kidnapped me, and now, I want to help him."

Cid then looked at Tubbs, who was sitting beside him.

"What, who—me?" Tubbs asked. "Is this how this works? We go around the circle?"

Cid shrugged his shoulders and said, "Yup."

"I'm Tubbs—called that because I'm a little bit tubby, I know. But for twenty years, I've sailed the great seas as a sailor in the Canadian Navy. I'm a master seaman; that's my rank. Yes, I'm going bald, and I've been around for a while. But heck, I can dispense a lot of good advice, and I'll help as best as I can to see us through this here adventure. A few days ago, I thought that my time was up, but I guess not, so here I am." Tubbs then looked around, scratched his nose, and sat down.

Stefan then stood up. "I'm Stefan a Petty Officer on a ship now laying fathoms below us. I'm a bit confused by all of this and saddened to have lost so many good friends. Still now we are here and we are alive so I am thankful for that. Let's getter done and put some trust in Mr. Scar and Cid. Then Stefan sat still looking a bit perplexed.

A middle-aged man then stood. He was stocky, had a chiseled look to his face, and wore a small cap. He folded his arms and announced, "I'm Darcy McTaggart, first mate on the schooner *Bounty's Fortune*. I'm from Cape Breton and sail out of Halifax now. I am surprised to find myself here. Like this Stefan fella, I am a bit confused by it all. But I have given my word, and I'll stand by it." He then looked around at the other men, nodded his head, and sat down.

Then the twins stood. They looked exactly alike; however, one wore a red cap and the other a green. Bill shared, "The fellow next to me in the red cap is Stan. He's my twin, if you haven't noticed."

That set the rest of the gathering laughing.

"Don't believe him; he's color blind," Stan said.

"Am not. I'm Bill. I'm the younger of us two, but I got the brains, and most of the good looks."

"We're twins, Bill. I think we share everything equally, anyway."

"We're from Newfoundland, and we sail with our dad. He's probably heartbroken at the moment, so we both are trusting in Mr. Scar's words."

Then they both slowly sat down, worry etched on their faces.

Redheaded Reggie then jumped up. "Hi. I'm Reggie, from the Avalon Peninsula. My family grows apples, but I decided I want to fish. So here I am, ready for this new adventure and willing to pitch in." Then he promptly sat back down.

A wiry fellow next stood up and looked around. "I'm Tazzle. I've been fishing for fifteen years out here on the Grand Banks. I've helmed many a ship. I even whaled in my first few years. I've been around the Cape, and I've been around the Horn, so if you need a good helmsman, here I am. Now, I ain't bragging. I'm just saying if you need me doing it, I'm here."

The last of the sailors stood. He was a medium-sized man in his mid-thirties with sandy brown hair and a quiet manner about him. "I'm Fred, and I'm a machinist. I know engines and how to make things work. I can help when you need those diesels working, but I'm willing to lend a hand sailing also. My mates and I are grateful to you for saving us. *Thanks* is all I can say."

Dan then stood up. "I'm the new kid on the block. My name is Dan, and I'm from Toronto, but I have spent a great deal of time on this boat looking after it. It's been in dry dock for some time being overhauled, and I am the night watchman. So, I basically have been dreaming about sailing on her, and now, here I am."

A tall, lumbering fellow stood up and squinched his face, most of which was hidden behind a beard. "I'm Josh. I do my job. I don't ask questions. I'm from Prince Edward Island, and I sail out of St. John's. Captain Eberheart is my captain. I'll work here with you and then expect to return to the good captain as soon as we're done."

"Trent's my name." Quickly, before Josh could sit, Trent jumped up. "Don't like to talk much. I'm from Newfoundland, like the twin boys. Thanks for having me aboard." Then he sat.

A broad-shouldered man quietly stood, removed his hat, and looked around at the room. "My name's Rupert. I'm from Antigonish, and I hope to get back there when all is said and done. Thank you all." With that, he put back his cap and quietly and slowly sat back down.

A lean-looking fellow with long blond hair then casually stood. "I'm Willy, and just like that, I'm willing to help us along. I'm from Cape Breton now, but I was born in British Columbia. I fished the West Coast, and then I ventured out here to the east. I will stay and sail this beautiful schooner and then go back home for a visit."

Scar looked at them all and smiled. "Thank you, mateys. Well, so our voyage begins. I'll work out a watch rotation. Each of you should sit down with me and tell me a bit about yourself and what you can do. Cid here is new to sailing, and he started the voyage with me. He's easily swayed by more mature and knowledgeable hands. I'd appreciate it if you helped him learn the ropes. I'll talk to each of you and figure out who would make a suitable first mate—who has the most experience with sailing a schooner. We'll split into two shifts: me in charge of one and whoever I pick in charge of the other. Four hours on and four hours off—I take that is standard."

A round of ayes came from the group.

"Good. I'll mingle a bit and ask each of you to tell me about yourselves. I'm a good judge of character, so I'll find someone suitable. Oh, and as a side note, we are going to run into pirates also."

"Pirates?" Tazzle's voice went a bit squeaky.

Scar spent the rest of the night explaining and interviewing. The man he picked for first mate was an experienced hand from Halifax who had an even temperament and knew schooner sailing quite well.

Darcy McTaggart was his name. He liked a pipe, and he had a twinkle in his eye and hands that had seen yards of work.

Scar liked Darcy. He had a voice that could carry on deck. The man was deep chested and clear in his speaking.

"I'll help you, Mr. Scar," Darcy said, "although I don't see to treating men meanly, only firmly, when things need to get done."

Scar looked him squarely in the eye and said, "You will do just fine." Then they shook hands and that was it; decided it was.

Dan loved the *Bluenose Two*. For two years, he had guarded her and had learned everything he could about her and her namesake's history. He had walked and touched every inch of the proud schooner. He had also dreamed of her sailing and seen himself riding the waves with her. He had dreamed of the original *Bluenose* and longed for that time and life.

Now here he was out on the ocean, sailing on the *Bluenose Two*, fulfilling his every dream. He had a smile as big as Scar's. He wandered about the ship, looking up at the great sail, and ran his hands on the rail. He couldn't figure out how this had happened, but for now, it didn't matter. She was doing what she was meant for, and he was with her.

Scar was watching Dan. A smile crossed his face. "He's part of the magic!" Scar said aloud.

"What's that?" Fred asked.

"Nothing but something good."

Meanwhile, Stefan leaned over the rail, his eyes searching the seas. He couldn't let the war go; the threat of submarines still held him hostage. For the last two years, he'd scoured the seas looking for periscopes. The fear still gripped him. How could they be outside of time? It didn't make any sense. And magic was another thing. *Really?* Yet here they all were. The crew all came from different time periods. He was on a ship that hadn't been built yet, sailing to find a bunch of actors from the past.

As he was puzzling over this and staring at the sea, he thought he saw a ship. *No way,* he said to himself. It was a Viking dragon boat. It was sailing west just barely out of sight. Then it disappeared.

"What was that?" Stefan asked.

"You talking to me?" Chappy replied as he came next to Stefan.

"I thought I saw a ship. It was strange. It looked like a Viking ship." With that, he scratched his head and rubbed his eyes.

"You might have," Chappy said.

"Come on." Stefan shook his head.

"Look, Scar said that we are outside of normal time. I think that time here is compressed and the past is joined with the present and maybe even the future. So things might come and go that we have trouble believing are really here. I mean all these fishermen from different years and even Dan. Dan is from the future."

"How can that be, Chappy?"

"I don't know. Right now, I'm just looking at what is in front of me and trusting that it will work out."

"Still, a Viking ship!" Stefan questioned.

"Too bad we can't get a picture of it, maybe an actual photo of Leif Erikson."

"Chappy, doesn't any of this throw you off? What about your spiritual—"

"Stefan, I'm still a chaplain, and I still hold to my beliefs. I know Scar looks to be a goblin. I don't judge a man by his looks, however. I judge him by his behavior, and even then, I can be forgiving, or at least I try to be understanding."

"You're a good man, Chappy."

"Thanks. Hang in there. Oh, if you see a monk in a little round boat, let me know, will you?" With that, Chappy set off to find Scar. He had something he needed to ask him. Stefan, meanwhile, watched Chappy leave with a puzzled look on his face.

Chappy found Scar near the aft section of the schooner. "Can I ask you a favor, Scar?"

"Sure. How can I be of service?"

"Exactly what I was thinking of."

"Huh?" Scar's puzzling look made Chappy laugh.

"A church service—you know, a Mass? Would it be all right if I share a Mass each Sunday with those who want to share in it?"

"That's fine with me, Chappy," Scar replied. "I respect your keen interest in the souls. It might even help them feel at home."

"Thank you, Scar. You know, I didn't expect that from a goblin."

"Appearances can be misleading. For instance, I didn't think that Dan there would turn out to be a musician."

"What are you talking about?" Chappy asked.

"Look over there."

Dan had emerged from below deck with a guitar, and smiling, he sat midship and began strumming. "I'm sure there are other musicians on board, but anyways, I remembered that this was down in the hold along with a harmonica and a few other musical instruments." With that, he played and sang a few folk songs.

The majority of the crew were elated, and those on deck who were not working gathered around Dan. Most of them had never before heard any of the songs he played.

"Well, here is one that maybe only Cid has heard before. It's about the namesake of this boat," Dan said.

Cid began to sing along to "Who Will Know the *Bluenose*" by Stan Rogers. The crew loved it and tried to join in on the chorus. The time spent singing and laughing and letting Cid entertain them turned into a happy day of sailing.

CHAPTER 8

THE NEXT MORNING FOUND THE *Bluenose Two* SAILING SOUTHWEST.
Cid was on deck, standing by the wheel. Last night, everything
seemed to be out of his hands. He had felt like an observer at a strange
event. Yet he was totally involved. How could they be outside of time?
That thought kept him puzzled.

Tazzle was the man at the wheel. He had come from a small fishing
village. He kept his eye on the horizon but began talking to Cid. "1857.
That's when I was born, in just a little village on Cape Breton. I started
fishing with my da when I was about thirteen. I just left the boat two
days ago, and now here I am, over a hundred years later."

"How long have you been fishing?"

"I think maybe twenty-two years. My da's a good man, fair and full
of laughter and a right hard worker. I'll take over for him someday. I
have to work hard to keep up with him, though." He smiled when he
said that, yet he looked like he might cry.

"I trust Scar. If he says he'll get you back, Tazzle, he will," Cid told
him. "I know that. I have no proof, but I can only trust my measure of
the man—I mean, goblin."

"Not much I can do about it, anyway, so let's sail and see what
turns up."

"I'll get you back, Tazz. I promise." Cid held his hand out to his
shipmate, and Tazzle gripped it with firmness.

"Just by doing that, you've made me feel more confident, Cid. I
trust a man who looks me in the eye and shakes my hand."

"So do I, Tazz." Cid knew he'd made a promise, and even if he didn't know how he would fulfill it, he knew he would give everything to accomplish it.

The crew spent the next few hours on a southwest heading. It was a beautiful, clear day, and the *Bluenose* took to the waves like a thoroughbred. Cid was thrilled as the ship raced through and over the waves. It felt like flying.

Chappy had been designated as the cook, a role that he took to with delight, as it gave him the chance to be free enough to see to everyone's spiritual well-being as well as their need for good wholesome food. The boat was well stocked, which was a miracle as far as Cid could figure.

Scar put the rest of the navy crew plus Cid, Tazzle, Bill, and Stan on his watch. Bill and Stan, the two Halifax brothers, could handle the sails with ease and help the navy boys and Cid learn the ropes rather fast. They were pretty good natured about it. Smiley had them all laughing continuously, so that first watch passed rather well.

Darcy's watch took over at noon, which gave Cid time to relax.

The next three days were spent sailing in glorious weather. Sailing was becoming routine. Cid was getting the hang of it all and enjoying the company of his fellow sailors. Dan was having the time of his life fulfilling his lifelong dream; he felt like he was standing in Angus Mcfee's shadow.

Tazzle, Stan, and Bill taught the new boys about hauling sails, tying knots, and climbing in the rigging. The twins were identical and could only be discerned because Bill wore a green bandana on his head and Stan wore a red one. Bill and Stan, at Darcy's request, spent hours teaching Dan and Cid how to tie various knots. They also taught them the names of the sails and the ropes and the parts of the ship aft and fore. Dan had a bit of a head start, so Cid had to pay attention and focus on remembering all the names.

The next few weeks were an endless routine of hauling on ropes, furling the giant sail, and hauling on more ropes. At times, the entire crew would all dash to the side of the boat as it leaned into the wind. At first, Cid was terrified that they would keel over, but the ship would right itself and fly across the water. It seemed that the days passed rather quickly, and no sooner did Cid drop into his bunk than he was up again, hauling on ropes and laughing with the men. Cid had to grapple with his fear of heights, but by focusing on the task at hand, somehow, he was managing it.

Whenever Scar was on deck, he grinned his wide goblin grin. As wonderful as his grin was, the men wondered about what was going on. Where were they in time? Had they been snatched from death? Would they return to their own times? Where were they going, really? None of them voiced these concerns, but all of them thought about them.

After two weeks of sailing, Darcy took the watch. The sky had been clear all night with a gentle breeze. The stars hung from the sky. A full moon looked down through the night and was now setting in the west. Morning came with a pink horizon that turned into a crimson red. It was a sailor's warning.

The gentle breeze picked up in intensity and by eight o'clock turned stronger. One check of the moon, it was there; the next moment, the moon was gone. A black mountain of clouds was climbing up the sky toward the ship. Darcy suddenly yelled, "All hands! Hurricane coming!" He then ran to the ship's bell and started clanging away.

Scar came on deck and stared at the clouds. "We'll head east and try to go around it!" Scar yelled toward Darcy. "Make sure everyone has survival gear on, and tie everyone to something that won't blow away."

The gallant ship raced to the east and seemed to be winning when the storm picked up more speed. The race was a foregone conclusion. "Too much sail! We need to lower the mainmast. We'll keep enough sail to maneuver," Darcy shouted to Dan. With that, the mainmast was lowered.

Cid had come up on deck bleary eyed from being in a deep sleep. One look at what was happening, and he jumped to help.

Then the storm was upon them. It took everything to just hold on. Cid found himself braced to the mast beside Scar. Scar was yelling to the crew. "All the sails will have to come down! This wind will rip them to shreds!"

"We can start up the diesels!" Dan shouted out.

"I forgot about the diesels. Get down there, Dan, and get them going! Grab Fred; he's a machinist, knows engines. We can use them to maneuver. Smart boy, that one." Scar punched Cid in the shoulder and grinned at him. "Hell, of a ride, eh?"

How the crew managed to survive, none of them could explain. At one point, they faced down what seemed to be a hundred-foot wave, and then they were thrust up a similar giant, and then the giant swirl spun them around its edge. To peer down was to see eternity, while looking up, one could only view dark walls of wave and dark walls of cloud. The howling of the wind was loud enough to drown out all other sound. In the end, they just held on.

Then it seemed that they were floating on air and cloud. It was surreal and silent, and out of the fog, ships from various ages emerged and disappeared—Viking ships and passenger liners, strange ships that resembled junks, warships, and odd, sleek tube-like creations. None of the crew could speak or be heard as all of this transpired, and then it stopped, and they were lying still on a silent sea.

It was then that Cid began to shake and doubts entered his mind. As this happened, the *Bluenose* shimmered and the *Little Bluenose* began to appear.

Scar screamed at Cid, "Stop that!" and slapped him. Cid shook his head, bewildered.

Cid was lost in a sense of surrealism, but then he thought that no word existed to describe how he felt. Images of Chris Hadfield floating in space and singing David Bowie's "Space Oddity" flashed through his mind. Nothing was familiar. He was lost in a dimensionless space of time and physicality. Scar's slap had left him disentangled, and he strove to get back to that moment like it was an anchor in time. For an endless moment, he felt like he was swimming and then without gravity.

At one point, Chris Hadfield was talking to him and telling him to get a grip on himself. Cid tried desperately. When he glanced up, however, he could see endless dark skies inside eternal walls of circular cloud. Then he saw that he was on top of a giant circular wave in some vast whirlpool, looking down into an endless vortex. Nausea threatened to overtake him, and finally, an inner voice told him to hang in there. All was cool, and he would survive.

Then he focused and saw Scar standing in front of him. Concern and fear were written all over Scar's face. This thought made Cid laugh. The words weren't really written on Scar's face, but the idea was present, and it cracked Cid up.

"Cid, Cid, get a hold of yourself. We need you, please." Scar held Cid's face in his hands and pleaded with him.

"I'm OK, I'm OK. Thanks, Scar."

Scar released Cid and then suddenly hugged him. "I'm sorry I've put you through this."

A sense of calm came over Cid. The ship was intact and still the *Bluenose Two*.

"Keep your eyes on the *Bluenose*. See the ship, the rigging, the mast. What color is the deck? Who is at the helm? Look at him. What's he wearing? Stay focused, Cid! You are the one holding the magic. It's you, so stay focused on it."

"OK. I'm all right, Scar." Cid began breathing and calmed down.

"Good lad. You had me scared there for a minute. The things you see out there aren't real—well, maybe they are, but they won't touch us or harm us. They are in a different time and are just passing us by."

Cid stared out at the sea.

CHAPTER 9

SERGEANT BARKER STOOD ON THE WHARF AT LUNENBURG. THE police tape kept any intruders from crossing and crawling over the little fishing boat occupying the spot where the *Bluenose* was supposed to be. Crowds were still hanging around, and newspeople still came and did stories about it. At this moment, three different camera crews were filming the little fishing boat. It served as the backdrop for two newscasters' evening reports. ABC and CBC both had stories on it that night.

Sergeant Barker found this assignment boring. A Royal Canadian Mounted Police (RCMP) officer should have more serious assignments. Still, switching the Bluenose with a tiny fishing boat bothered him. How had the crooks pulled it off? How had they stolen a national treasure and replaced it with a silly fishing boat? In the back of his mind, he thought that some celebrity had done this as a prank and that he was going to be on camera looking like a silly twit when the gag was aired.

Taking a breath, he relaxed and looked again at the *Little Bluenose*. At that moment, the boat shimmered and the *Bluenose Two* appeared with a full crew on board, looking severely distressed. As shocking as this was, the sight of the gray goblin distressed him the most.

Barker dropped his coffee. All he could think was that he was going crazy.

He discovered that he wasn't crazy, however, because shortly after the *Bluenose Two* disappeared again and the *Little Bluenose* reappeared, the camera crews started screaming that they had it all on tape.

CHAPTER 10

I'M SORRY I'VE PUT YOU THROUGH THIS."

A sense of calm came over Cid. The ship was intact and still the *Bluenose Two*.

"What happened?"

Scar leaned into Cid and spoke quietly. "Cid, never lose your faith in what we are doing. You hold the magic that keeps this together. I believe in you, and I am trusting in you to keep it together. An actor's belief, remember. Stage magic is what this is, and you have it. This ship is here because you keep it here. If you waver, then it will be lost. I'm counting on you, and all these lives now depend on you. The show must go on and all that stuff. Don't lose it!" Scar leaned back and looked deeply into Cid's eyes. "You are saving lives, and this is the greatest performance of your whole life. This one matters the most. This performance is real. No one is going to believe it but me and you and the men around you. Don't drop the ball!"

Cid shook himself and then gripped a handhold and looked around at the ship. Members of the crew were staring at him in the way that only old mariners could. So, Cid did what any true mariner would do at that moment. He looked at Scar, grinned back, and said, "Skipper, I think that we could all use a bit of grog at this moment."

Shouts of "Aye, the lad's got it right" and "Spoken like a true mariner" and various ayes and yeses and yahoos were shouted. Scar beamed an even brighter smile, and soon, a jar of rum was being passed around and all hands were on deck, laughing and smiling.

The rest of the day passed in a lazy sail with the occasional phantom boat passing by or passing overhead or even passing below. It was unusual and unsettling, but the crew for the moment just enjoyed one another's company and took to the task of simply sailing. The storm had gone as quickly as it had arrived.

Later that evening, Scar thanked Cid for staying calm and told him that it had been a close call. "'Twas the Triangle," he said ominously. "And it was a storm of fantastical proportions and elements, the type that Shakespeare refers to in *The Tempest*, except this one was a dimensional one because it crossed time and place. They're hard to figure out, and our messing with time could have triggered this one. All those ships were real, but they were out of sync in the time dimensions."

Cid just nodded his head in agreement. He thought that the rum was messing with his mind or with Scar's, or it was all true and he just couldn't grasp it at this time.

In the end, he just went to his bunk and slept it off. Sailing being what it is, he was up at four and back on the deck for his watch.

CHAPTER 11

F ROM A SHELTERED COVE ON A LONG-FORGOTTEN ISLAND IN THE South Pacific, a ship with dark sails eased its way out of the harbor. The island couldn't be found on any chart, nor had any mariner come across it—at least not since the present ship had taken residence there. The ship flew the skull and crossbones proudly; for centuries, it had plied its trade. Its one purpose now was but to find one boat.

The captain had one purpose, and that intent had driven him to outlast time and death and cling to a hope of destroying one enemy. He was chasing a ship of fools. These fools had humiliated the black ship's captain. Revenge was all he wished for and lived for and lingered in a quasi-limbo world seeking. His crew trusted him out of fear and awe. None of them loved him, but all of them followed him because he was their anchor in their demented, fearful, angry existence.

Lusic was all he was known as—Captain Lusic, who some once called the devil. Scaramouche was his bane, his forever hated target. He had escaped him somehow. So, he had gone after his company of actors, and they, too, had escaped him. Next in line was Scaramouche's friend Moliere. Lusic had tried to kill Moliere but had failed and had followed his acting company after Moliere's death with the idea of murdering every last one of them. He would enact his revenge if it took him eternity. But he had lost them. Somewhere, they had boarded a ship and sailed away from France.

That was hundreds of years ago, and still, Lusic pursued them. He had schemed his way onto a ship and plotted and manipulated his way until finally he had gotten rid of the captain and any honest-intentioned sailors and had taken over the ship himself. Then he had captured a small frigate and taken it over. That was what he had used to pursue his enemies. By pirating, he had attracted a crew that fit his schemes. He had become a legend of tyranny, hundreds of years following his instincts, constantly pursuing his prey. Now, his instincts led him forth, and out he came, slinking into the open ocean. Sails unfurled, and the pursuit began again.

He was a presence, a feeling. He commanded by intent and very few words. What words he used were pointed and direct. He always seemed to be in a black swirl, but there was never much movement around him except in moments of violence. Two henchmen were always with him. They always stood on either side of him, the menacing one smiling and the other scowling. Either was terrifying, but combined with Lusic, they were overwhelming in their ability to cause fear. They were the ones who saw that Lusic's commands were carried out. The rest of the crew were lost souls trapped in their allegiance to such an evil leader either by fear or by greed or by both.

"I feel a presence; someone new has joined the prey." Lusic rubbed his cheek and grinned.

Gratso, the smiling one, replied, "Where?"

"Sail due east, till we reach Easter Island"

"Aye, Captain."

The captain leaned out over the rail, staring into the water. His thoughts turned back, looking at the past.

He had loved her. She never should have married that buffoon. He was not good enough for her, and when their affair had been discovered, the buffoon had sent her to a nunnery. Lusic had tried everything to get her back, but nothing worked. He had never seen her again. When everything he tried failed, he had resorted to this. He pursued the buffoon, seeking revenge. Now, he knew that he was out there on the ocean, coming nearer. The buffoon was out there.

"I will find you this time," Lusic growled out loud.

His hands on the rail, he stood still, facing the horizon. Flanking him were his two henchmen, his eternal guards. As darkness came on, they remained in position, staring into the dark.

CHAPTER 12

THE *BLUENOSE TWO* HAD BEEN SAILING FOR A COUPLE OF WEEKS, now having skirted the Caribbean. She was on a southern heading following the South American coast, headed for the Straits of Magellan. It was the kind of sailing the *Bluenose* had been built for. She took to the water and sailed clean and fast. The crew enjoyed this time and settled into rounds of work, each jumping into the tasks. Many a day they spent working and singing and laughing and sleeping the joyful sleep of work done hard and honestly.

Cid was happy. The views were awe inspiring. The mood of the crew was happy. The routine of work had a comfort all its own. This led Cid to relax and trust what was going on, so much so that after crawling into his cot one night, he quickly went into a deep, dream-filled slumber.

In the dream, he was at home, where he'd grown up. Out on the downtown street, people were coming out of the movie theater.

I've been here before.

Nobody looked closely at him. They just walked around him, ignoring him. A rush of people—lots of people—were laughing and talking with one another, and all were heading somewhere. He felt like a stone in a stream with everyone washing around him.

Then he saw the three walking toward him. Lusic was in the middle, and on either side of him were his thugs. One was taller, slick, with shoulder-length hair; the other was shorter with sandy hair. Lusic always seemed to carry a dark presence—short black hair, leather jacket, everything neat and orderly.

Lusic began a conversation about how Cid had mentioned buying dope from the Greasers while he was onstage at the coffeehouse a few nights ago. He pointed out how offensive this was to him and his friends. Cid was lost, puzzled, terrified.

How he had gotten onstage at the coffeehouse was something that Cid could not figure out. What the heck had happened? Why had he started talking and singing and performing? Why had he done that? None of it made any sense. Not only had it been a bad performance, but he had caught the wrath of Lusic, who at this moment was slapping Cid around and threatening his very existence.

Somehow, the crowd failed to diminish or take any notice of what was going on. In the end, Cid stood there alone, terrified, his life now having been given a notice of termination. After threatening Cid, Lusic and his two goons walked away.

Cid woke up. It had been a dream, but Cid knew that it had also happened to him just like the dream. The memory was as clear as when it had happened. The terror took some time to abate. *At least,* he thought, *that is now just a memory.*

On a dark ship on the Pacific, Lusic smiled, not a happy smile but a smile. "Now I remember you."

CHAPTER 13

TIERRA DEL FUEGO—CID COULDN'T BELIEVE THAT THEY WERE almost upon it. Soon, they would be approaching the Straits of Magellan. Up until now, these had all been names on a map, but now, here they were.

Chappy came sauntering over to him.

"Was through here three years ago. Cruisin' on a frigate, the *HMS Frobisher.* Captain warned us of gales, but it being power driven by diesels, the winds never bothered us. Many a sailboat has had a tough time here, though. It's worse if you go south and try Drake's Pass." He just leaned on the rail and stared at the mountains after that. "Patagonia."

"Yes."

"Did you ever hear the story about the giants that lived there?"

"I did, but it was never proven to be true. Still, I like unsolved mysteries."

Chappy grinned at him then and patted Cid on the shoulder. "Maybe the winds will be kind to us."

They weren't; in fact, they seemed to ignore Chappy's suggestion. Two days into the straits, the gales began. The problem was the gales couldn't decide on which direction they wished to blow from.

For three days, the crew lay in a cove hoping the anchors would hold and waiting out the bashing. For some reason, Dan found this to be terribly exciting and spent the entire three days above deck, gawking at the waves and the drenched shoreline and excitedly yelling about how gorgeous it all was. The rest of the crew admired his enthusiasm and secretly thanked him for keeping their spirits up. Most of the time, they teased him good naturedly and carried on with whatever tasks they could in the soaking conditions.

Below deck was incredibly miserable for those trying to find calmness and solitude. Everything was turbulent, so much so that hanging on for dear life was the only common thread. Scar just kept calm; he told everyone repeatedly that it would all pass soon and they would make headway when the winds died down.

Finally, when the stress of rain, rain, and more rain was approaching the last-straw moment, the sky cleared and the sun came out. The wind simply stopped, and all was calm.

Scar hopped up on deck and smiled. "Guess we'll have to use those diesels." The diesel engines were put to use for the second time, and they chugged their way through the straits.

It took three days, but the scenery was spectacular. Cid indulged himself and with pencils and pads spent most of the time sketching the mountains and scenery as well as his fellow shipmates.

"They're good," Scar commented while scanning through Cid's pads. "You have some talent there. I'd keep it up if I was you. Definitely have a dramatic flair."

"Sketching has helped keep my love of acting alive," Cid replied.

"Huh?"

"Well … creating a role starts with a sketch, and then you fill in the details, little bits at a time. I seem to do my best work when I capture a dramatic moment, and that seems to have come naturally."

"I get it, and yes, I agree. I'd love to see you act in a play, but then, who knows what life will bring to you."

"That would be great. However, as far as adventures go, this is quite something. The scenery here is incredible."

CHAPTER 14

SOMEWHERE NEAR SAINT INÉS, THE CREW WAS CALLED ON DECK. Darcy's rich baritone voice called, "All hands." Everyone had been sleeping in their clothes. The mainsail had to be taken in. All hands were needed.

Cid felt like his hands were ice as he labored alongside Stefan and Smiley. Slowly and methodically, they rolled the canvas and tied it in place. Stefan grinned at Cid. The crew had become a team, and they all pulled together to do the work. They had become a family in a sense. Cid was enjoying himself on one level. On another level, he was wet, sore, and scared out of his mind. When the sails were hauled in, the watch was released, and Cid managed somehow to find his bunk.

Moments later, Stefan aroused him. "Our watch."

Cid went on deck as fast as he could. Scar had the helm. Dawn was just beginning. The winds had died down, and that meant more sail could be put on. Cid climbed into the rigging with the other hands, careful not to step on the running rigging. As a team now, they climbed out on the yards and unfurled the sails. The heights weren't bothering Cid as much as when he first did this. Smiley always stayed close to him and helped build his confidence. On deck, pulling on the halyards to set the sails, most of them now sang in unison as they pulled.

Chappy had become the cook and was excelling at the task. So, while the rest of the crew toiled at sail raising and lowering, Chappy nurtured their souls and stomachs.

One day, it happened. They reached the Pacific. It was a beautiful day. Cold winds blew from the southeast. The ship responded to the winds like a thoroughbred and sailed fast and clean. All hands came up and enjoyed the experience.

Scar announced that they would sail within sight of the coast and then in a few days head west toward the Easter Islands.

Two days out from the coast, Scar asked Stefan, Chappy, and the three other navy men to join Cid and him in the hold.

"Why down here, Scar?" Stefan asked.

"I need you to see this," Scar explained, and he pointed to a large crate. "I need you to open this up and assemble it." He looked at Stefan.

"What is it?" Cid was finding all of this oddly concerning.

"It's a cannon. Try not to get concerned."

"Why?" chimed in Chappy.

"Remember the pirates I mentioned that first night?" They all perked up and stared at Scar. "We are about to meet them. Maybe not today, but soon. I want to be ready for them with a bit of a surprise."

"Is this for real?" Stefan asked, rubbing his face and sighing.

Cid began to honestly feel frightened.

"Yes, and I need you to be really good with this cannon. We can't kill the pirates. I don't even know if they are alive. However, their ship is real, and it can be disabled if hit properly."

Chappy looked at Scar in shock. "Not alive!"

"I'm not sure. They have been around as long as I have. Same crew and same captain."

"How long is that?" Cid asked.

"Do all of you know who Moliere was?" Everyone shrugged and shook their heads. "How about the Sun King?"

Cid hadn't reacted mainly because he was grappling with the first question. "Moliere? You were with Moliere?"

"Best of friends. This pirate is after me and my friends, and has been chasing us since Moliere's time."

"Why?" Cid asked.

"I wronged him. And as sorry as I am for doing what I did, he has carried on this obsession far too long."

"We're talking centuries!" Cid exclaimed.

56

"Yes, a bit over the top, don't you think?"

"Why?" asked Chappy.

"Revenge."

The others all stood there in shock.

"Let me tell you a story. Back in the day, Mother Church frowned upon actors. In fact, actors were not allowed to be buried in sacred ground. That was a bad call, as everyone at that time in that place was Roman Catholic. My friend Moliere, when he died, was not allowed to be buried in sacred ground. Finally, the king had to beg permission from the pope, who allowed it on one condition. The condition was that none of Moliere's actors would ever be allowed to be buried in sacred ground. My friends were cursed to eternity in Limbo. I am trying to save them, and that is why we are on this journey."

Stefan shook his head. "Terrible story, but that doesn't explain the pirates."

"I wronged the captain of that ship, even though I thought that I was in the right." Scar looked sheepishly at the floor and seemed to be struggling with something. Then he looked up. "OK, here's what happened. I thought that my wife was having an affair, so I had her committed to a nunnery. The man besides myself who loved her vowed revenge. He could never achieve it. I always thwarted him. I went to England and performed there and kept performing until I was very old. My wife put a curse on me. That is why I am a goblin. I wasn't always. By saving my friends, I may be able to lift the curse. Hopefully, the pirates won't prevent me from accomplishing this."

Everyone just stared at Scar.

Smiley scratched his head and then looked at Scar really closely. "Is this all true, Scar?"

"All of it. I was very famous. I had my own acting company, and I performed for many years, until I was quite old. Then when I thought that my time was up, instead of having a curtain call, I turned into a goblin."

Chappy shook his head. "That is just weird. I mean, that is really hard to accept."

"Believe me, Chappy, it was even harder for me."

Cid piped in. "This enemy of yours …"

"His name is Lusic."

"What?" Cid felt his heart stop. "Who did you say?"

"Lusic."

"I know him. He threatened to kill me. I said bad things about him while performing at a coffeehouse."

Scar stared at Cid. "He has you marked. I don't know how he did it, but he connected the dots. Somehow, time is not an issue with him either. My acting company and Moliere's, if you can believe it, are on a ship. They have been doomed to spend eternity sailing in Limbo. None of them could be buried in sacred ground and this became their curse. I am going to save them. I am going to find them and bring them somewhere that they can finally rest. I will also take care of my nemesis. This revenge thing has gone on for much too long. All I can say is we will use this gun to stop his ship or slow him down. I think that the *Bluenose* can outsail anything, and we will have to trust that she can save us."

Stefan piped in, "Let's get this gun up on deck, then, and find a useful spot to place her. We'll have to try a few rounds out just so that we get used to her."

With that, the seamen hauled the gun up on deck. Luckily, the *Bluenose* was equipped to lift large fishholds from below, so with some rope and tackle, the men were able to maneuver it up. It was a strange sort of gun, however. It was a cannon, but it seemed to have big gas canisters attached to it. The ammo was giant balls that were all different colors. The balls were placed in hard sleeves that attached to the side of the gun.

Some of the crew expressed concerns over having a gun on deck. Scar told them of its intended use and assured everyone that no one would be killed using it. No one seemed fully convinced of this, however.

CHAPTER 15

T WO DAYS LATER, THEY WERE FURTHER OUT IN THE PACIFIC ON A northwest heading, and the winds were ice cold. Everyone was bundled up, doing what they could to stay warm. Bill and his brother joined Cid, and both were commenting on the cold.

"Winds from Antarctica," Bill said with great certainty.

"Has to be when it's that cold," Stan chimed in.

Cid nodded in agreement. "It's brutal."

"It will get warmer as we head north." Stan sounded reassuring.

Cid looked at him and scrunched his face. "I'm not sure we are heading north."

"Where we headed?" Bill looked Cid in the eye.

"From what I gather, west out there somewhere."

"The Easter Islands are out there. Is he thinking of taking us to Japan?"

"No, I don't think so." Cid felt uncertain. Uncertainty had been bothering him for a bit, ever since the cannon had been introduced. "He mentioned an island not found on the maps."

"Geez, Cid, that is not encouraging." Bill shrugged his shoulders and stared off into the west.

"Sail ho!" Reggie had a keen eye and was aloft at that moment.

Darcy, standing amidships, yelled up to him, "Where, Reggie?"

"Northwest. Black sails and hard to see."

All hands came running, Scar among them. "It's him." He started pacing back and forth. "We need to prepare for a race. Set the sails, and let's try to shake him off."

The *Bluenose* was a born racer, and the ship lived up to its namesake. Throughout the day, she sped along, racing toward the horizon. As nightfall approached, they could see that the black sail had not come any closer.

Night came upon them. Scar had them change direction and sail northeast, hoping the black sail would follow the direction they had been heading.

It was a tense night. The men worried. Chappy fed them, but the men were silent. No one joked. No one spoke.

It was Smiley who came through for them. He started going around to each man, cheering them up in any way he could. He talked about little things and ordinary things and pets that he once owned. It was the bravest thing Cid had ever seen.

When dawn arrived, all eyes searched the horizon. Dan saw it first. "Black sail, southwest, and she's closer." He then stood at the rail and pointed.

"Good eyes!" one of the men exclaimed.

"She's gaining on us." Scar was standing with Chappy and the sailors. "I'm going to need you men to handle the howitzer. Chappy, I need you to bless the ammo with holy water."

"That seems odd to me, Mr. Scar."

"That is an ungodly boat, Chappy, and holy water will have an effect."

"Can't see how. And I thought that you said no one was going to be killed."

"No one will. Trust me."

"We're firing a cannon at a ship."

"Those men might not even be alive."

"Then why are we firing a cannon at them?"

"Because that is how you deal with pirates, You fire cannons at them!"

Cid spoke up. "What did you just say, Scar?"

"We are dealing with something nasty here, boys. That ship is cursed. Holy water is the only thing that will deter them. I aim to disable the ship and then fly before them and lose them as they try to repair their ship."

"With a cannon."

"Yes. A cannon with special artillery. Trust me; you will see."

"Do you want all the ammo blessed?" Chappy piped in.

"Yes. Maybe the gun itself, just for safety's sake."

The black ship appeared to be gaining.

"I think maybe by late afternoon, she'll be upon us. What we will do is when it gets close enough, we will turn and face it. When we are close enough to see them smiling, we will open up and aim to dismast them. After that, we will flee and get the heck out of here."

Cid thought the plan was harebrained and probably wouldn't work. But then again, it might be insane enough to actually do the trick. The truth of the matter was it was a crazy situation and a crazy idea was probably the only solution.

"I want you sailor boys manning the cannon. I can't let you try some ranging shots, because I don't want to give away our surprise."

Stefan, Tubbs, Smiley, and Fred went over to the gun and threw a big tarp over it. Then they crawled under the tarp and started fussing over it. Tubbs held up one end of the tarp so they could get some light.

The rest of the crew set about adjusting the sails, which mainly consisted of pulling on ropes whenever Scar gave them a command. For four hours, they watched the black ship gain on them.

Time was passing as the black ship neared. A safe distance slowly began to erode. The sailors were still under the tarp, preparing for their big moment.

It was late afternoon. The black ship was near enough to be able to pick out the pirates on the deck. They had brought a cannon onto their deck and fired off a warning shot. A plume of water erupted aft of the *Bluenose*.

"We are just out of range!" Darcy yelled from the wheel.

"Now!" yelled Scar. "Haul on those ropes. Hard a-port!"

Darcy spun the wheel, and the ship spun away, turning with the wind. All hands flattened themselves as the great sails tilted toward the sea. The ship nearly keeled over but once turned toward the black ship promptly righted itself.

Stefan and the boys threw off the tarp and began sighting the cannon. In a matter of a few minutes, the black ship was nearly upon them and began opening its gunports. The cannon barked a loud, thunking boom, and a giant splash of paint splattered the forecastle of the black ship.

Tubbs called out, "Higher, Stefan. Let's try a ranging shot."

The cannon barked out again, and this time, the mainmast erupted in color. Then the cannon barked for a third time, and the man at the helm was felled along with the wheel. A giant gush of paint erupted where he had been standing. The ship's steering went awry, and all the pirates paused and stood staring. A giant cracking sound split the momentary silence, and the great mainmast abruptly toppled over. The pirate ship was in disarray, its captain covered in blessed paint; its mainmast spreading its paint-covered sails over the sides of the ship, blinding the gunners; and its steering helm slathered with paint. The sailors whooped with glee and fired repeated shots, drenching the black ship with various paint colors. The *Bluenose* sailed past and left the pirate ship behind.

The black ship was in disarray. Sailors were slipping and tumbling. Cannons were all akimbo and facing in every direction. Sails were drooping and dripping, and the boat itself was circling with no sense of direction. Suddenly, the anchor dropped, and the ship came to a halt.

CHAPTER 16

ON BOARD THE PIRATE SHIP, LUSIC SEETHED. HE RANTED AND RAVED at his men. His two henchmen tried to stay clear of his tantrums and, in turn, screamed indignities at the rest of the crew.

Paint was everywhere. It burned to touch and steamed in the air as its holy-water makeup evaporated. Lusic knew repairing the ship and cleaning off the paint would take time. He stood at the rail and with hate-filled eyes watched the *Bluenose* sail away. He would find it again soon enough, and then he would punish those on board.

He would also find the other ship—the one he was always hunting, the one he knew was a ship of fools. It had been his lure. He knew that eventually, the buffoon would try to save the crew. The buffoon was just another fool, and soon, he would be rid of the fools. He'd make them suffer. He would make the buffoon suffer the most. He had plans for the buffoon and excruciating ways to deliver them. That thought was one of the few things that made Lusic smile.

Stefan and the sailors were whooping and hollering over their success, and the whole ship's crew laughed and cheered. Soon enough, however, they were busy hauling the ropes and sailing as fast as they could away from the encounter.

Scar had them sail north, and then once they were out of sight of the pirate ship, they turned toward the sunset and sailed west.

"Where to now, Scar?" Cid asked of him.

"We seek the Great Abyss. It's somewhere west of here. And before we reach it, I'm hoping we find my friends."

CHAPTER 17

THE *FORLORN HOPE* WAS A PRETTY LITTLE SHIP. IT HAD THE FEEL OF a gypsy caravan. Its sails were colorful and neatly trimmed, yet its course seemed erratic. It wandered in a somewhat aimless direction. Its crew handled it well, but they had become directionless. They sailed and put on plays for themselves and entertained each other, but it had become meaningless. They were a crew of actors sailing on the high seas, hoping to land in a harbor where they could perform. They were cursed to wander forever, never landing anywhere, never able to perform. Actors, however, are dreamers, and hope springs eternal even for the doomed. Their existence had become an eternity of waiting. When they weren't rehearsing, they would all just stare at one another with quiet, vacant eyes. So, the pretty little ship sailed on in an endless circle, going nowhere.

Giovanni stared out at the ocean—endless ocean. He was stretching while he stared, using the ship's rail like a dancer's bar. Why he was doing this, he wasn't sure. He always had to be ready to be flexible, he told himself, because someday, he would have to perform for an audience.

He would take anything—any ship, any port, he thought. The endless boredom was what got to him. If only something would come along to change the monotony.

He was watching a ship sailing way out in the distance. *That's a pretty ship,* he said to himself. *I bet they are having a wonderful time, free from boredom. I wish it was really there and I wasn't imagining it.* He paused. He stared. He jumped up and down, screaming about a ship.

Soon, the whole ship was screaming—perhaps not the ship, but the crew were dancing and shouting and kissing and shouting, and then they shouted and danced and kissed some more. They kept up with the merriment right until the *Bluenose* reached them. As it sidled up beside them, they all went silent and just stood there smiling and wiping tears from their eyes.

Scar waved to them. He had a big goblin grin. "Good day. I've been told that you want an audience with me."

Giovanni paused and then smiled. He stood on the railing and bowed. "We would be happy just to have an audience."

"We are here. First, we should talk, and then make plans to sail west of here. I'm afraid that we might have to hurry because there is a very nasty pirate chasing us." With that, Scar had the fishermen secure the two ships together and then set about introducing his crew to the actors.

Giovanni was somewhat taken aback by all of this. "How do you know us, Mr. Scar?"

"Ah, Giovanni, you might not remember. It was I that caused you this great banishment to the seven seas."

"No, no, that could not have been your fault. It was after Scaramouche had his falling-out with his wife."

"Yes, it was. That was me. Giovanni, it is me, Tiberio. I have been cursed and I have regretted my terrible crime, and I seek forgiveness from you. I seek redemption."

"Fiorilli, I don't understand."

"I am Tiberio."

"No, no, Tiberio is dead."

"I am not. I am cursed."

"But ..." Giovanni looked dazed.

"Maria cursed me, and rightfully so."

"How?"

"Women and a powerful anger. She was in the right, and I was in the wrong. Somehow, I became a goblin, and I have been searching for you to save you from this endless nightmare. I had to find something right to do. Lusic, her lover, however, has been chasing me all these years. He first wants to destroy you, my happy troupe. He wants to destroy anything that I valued. He is relentless. So, I am here to save you."

"Again, Mr. Fiorilli. Wait, you are Scaramouche."

With that, Giovanni started jumping about, and immediately, all the actors and actresses were jumping about and kissing each other and Scar and the sailors. Wine suddenly appeared, and big sausages and cheese and bread. Where those things came from was anyone's guess, but then, actors are so unpredictable.

Scar and Giovanni shared stories of their past, and Lucilla added some in. Giovanni formally introduced all the troupe, including a fair number of Moliere's troupe, who told the story of suddenly appearing on this boat, not knowing how or why they arrived here. Moliere's troupe seemed to consist of four beautiful women—one being Molier's wife, Armande Brejart. Miss Herve and Miss Brie introduced themselves, followed by two male actors: Brecourt, a regal personality, and Pa Croisy. These seemed to be the main actors.

Among Scar's troupe, Giovanni was large and loud and full of laughter. Pietro was smaller and incredibly flexible and full of mischief. Rembranto was perfectly in the middle of the other two, smaller than Giovanni and slightly taller than Pietro. Next was a tall, thin, quiet man, Doso, who obviously was Pierrot, the quiet zany one. Flippo and Buffalo bowed and accused each other of being zany. Lucilla bowed and did several flips and gymnastic extensions and then stopped and curtsied, revealing a stillness and beauty with her pleasant smile. Columbina then stepped out and regally gave her hello. Her beauty was unstoppable. A pause followed her introduction, and the crew of the *Bluenose* started to breathe again.

The crew of the *Bluenose* then all introduced themselves. Scar stood and, looking at the actors, stated, "It was that horrible pope. He cursed all of you. He wouldn't let you rest in hallowed ground. So, eternity is where you have been doomed to, sailing on an endless sea that leads to nowhere. But that is why I am here. I am going to figure out a way to end this. We shall have a great curtain call and then drop the curtain."

The actors, having found a willing audience, performed an impromptu show much to the delight of the fishermen and the sailors. Much song and wine were shared, and laughter and dancing went on way into the evening.

CHAPTER 18

THE NEXT MORNING FOUND THE TWO SHIPS SAILING WESTWARD. Scar was standing by the *Bluenose*'s wheel. Cid was at the helm.

"Hold her steady, Cid …"

"Land ho!" The shout came from Dan, who was pointing to the east. "Looks like a volcano—a really big volcano."

"That's it!" Scar cheered. "We found it!"

By now, all the crew had come on deck and were pointing and shouting. On the *Forlorn Hope*, everyone was dancing and shouting also.

It took them all a few hours to reach the island, and surprisingly, there was a small bay with a wharf for them to ease up to and anchor their ships.

"What now?" Cid was looking at Scar. "This island is a tremendously big volcano!"

Scar smiled. "It is the Great Abyss! You won't find it on any charts, but I knew it was here."

"What are we going to do here?"

"Climb to the top," Scar said. "Everyone, grab some food and whatever you need to make merry and have a picnic. We are going up to the top to celebrate everything."

That announcement seemed to galvanize the actors, who cheerfully exited their ship laden with picnic baskets, blankets, and anything musical that they could carry. This, of course, thoroughly excited the sailors, who grabbed whatever they could to add to the festivities.

Up the mountain they all trudged. At first, the going was exuberant, but gradually, it got exhausting, and later—much later—downright excruciating. Still, they continued to climb till finally they reached the top, where they all plunked down.

It had been an exhausting climb. So now as they sat there, they stared at the view, which was breathtaking. They could see for hundreds of miles, and most of it was ocean. The little bay where they had docked their ships seemed very tiny and far away.

Behind them was a gigantic cavernous hole. The Great Abyss was a huge volcano, its cone reaching far into the sky, and they were atop it. There was a path that led right around the top of the volcano; at most, the rim was three feet wide, and at least, a mere foot. Surrounding this lip was a calmer slope for about ten feet or more that followed the path all the way around the top. Then it was just mountain except for the trail that they had followed to get here.

The crater at times was steaming. To look down was like staring into eternity; it seemed endless. As they all crept to the edge and peered over, gasp or sigh in bewilderment was all they could do.

Then Scar stood up and invited them all to stand. "Right, let's not waste any time here. We have a job to do." He looked at them all, hands on his hips, and added, "Stand up, everyone!" They all did. "Let's spread out along the path."

Then they lined up along the path, the actors jumping right to it and the sailors and fishermen following suit in a somewhat confusing manner. They were all spread out now.

"Mr. Scar," Chappy nervously said, his hand shakily pointing at the Abyss, "it's quite high up here."

Scar laughed and bowed and then commented, "Yes, it is, and it's a great place to dance." With that, he made a bombastic bow and quacked like a duck. This, in turn, prompted Lucilla to bow with a bigger flourish and quack like a bigger duck. Next, Brecourt, not to be outdone, quacked like a duck and jumped in the air and did two bows. Cid, seeing all of this, suddenly spun like a top, bowed and quacked like a duck, and brayed like a donkey.

Soon, the foolishness was continuing down the line, and each subsequent actor, sailor, or fisherman topped the person before them. Then they all started to dance and twirl and spin their way around the top of the mountain. It was total nonsense and wacky and downright rude and hilarious. The dancing was outrageous. It took them around the top of the mountain until they came to where they had started. And Buffalo topped his gyration with a loud burp-like sound, only to top himself by the mountain, belching out an even more tremendous belch. This caused everyone to stop and break into hilarious laughter. Then they broke out the wine and food and danced and dined and sang and hugged and had a thoroughly good time together.

CHAPTER 19

AT THE BOTTOM OF THE MOUNTAIN, A BLACK PIRATE SHIP DOCKED. Lusic was seething. His men hurriedly left the ship and headed up the mountain. "No one stays on the ship," he announced. "We go to the top, and we deal with these fools."

The pirates, with grim determination, set off up the mountain. Their anger was evident. As a group, they resented the embarrassment of their last confrontation. It showed in their determination to get at their prey.

Lusic came behind, quiet and inwardly raging. Now, he had the object of his centuries-long resentment. Today, he would dish out his revenge.

They marched up the steep incline. It was a very steep incline, and after a few hours, they reached about a third of the way up, and all were panting and sweating and at times crawling as they climbed. By halfway, some of them were collapsing and needing to rest. This further infuriated Lusic, but even he was gasping for air. Perhaps their eagerness to reach their prey had overexerted them. They stood there for some time, catching their breath and panting.

"When we get there, I am going to kill them," Lusic wheezed. "Give me some water."

Gratso looked to Gritso, who shrugged, "We didn't bring any, boss."

Lusic stared out to the sea. "Let's get moving."

73

Stefan first saw the pirates approaching. He stood up and pointed. "Wow, that sure looks like an exhausted group."

Tubbs joined him. "They look wiped out, and I bet they're pretty thirsty."

Miss Brejart also looked at them. "I like their costumes. Very realistic."

Bill and Stan stood up, and Stan commented, "That's those pirates."

Scar stepped up to the path and raised his arms. "Hey, everyone, let's stand up here and welcome them!"

This caused a bit of confusion, but they all stepped up and joined Scar.

The pirates, upon entering the top, seemed confused. They were exhausted and could barely catch their breath.

Lusic sort of stumbled into the spot, and bent over and panted and tried to catch his breath. Then he straightened up and screamed, "I came here to kill you!"

"It's been a while," replied Scar.

"I've waited centuries, I have searched for you all this time, and you just greet me with a big smile?"

"Here I am. I must tell you that I am sorry for what has happened."

"Sorry you ruined my life—you ruined the love of my life? I loved her."

"Yes, and I am sorry. I truly am. It became my curse."

"I am too exhausted to bring you down to the ship and make you walk the plank."

"Why not let me do it here?"

"What?" Confusion clouded Lusic's face.

"Here. I will walk the plank here." And with that, Scar turned and stepped into the Abyss.

Everyone was shocked and stood as if in a daze.

Fred shouted out, "He just stepped into the Abyss!"

Lusic screamed, "That's not it. That doesn't make me feel any better. I want my revenge, and this is too easy. Kill all of them now!"

As he was saying this, each of the actors proceeded to backflip, somersault, and dive into the Abyss. The sailors and fishermen dove in after them in an attempt to save them or join them. None of them followed any rational thought. It was all impulse.

The pirates just stood there, looking over the edge.

CHAPTER 20

C ID FOUND HIMSELF WALKING. HE WAS ON A PLATFORM AT A TRAIN station. He recognized it from his childhood. A train was approaching. It chugged into the station, and its brown bear logo stood out. As it stopped, the engineer stuck his head out the window and said, "Hi, son!"

"Dad!"

"Your mum's here."

Cid looked down the train and saw her. Mum stood on the steps to one of the cars, holding two babies in her arms. She wore a flowery dress and reminded him of one of the Andrews Sisters.

"Mum, I have names for the babies."

"I know. We've been expecting you. Come closer and tell me their names."

Cid approached his mom and whispered their names. She smiled a radiant, loving smile.

"Dad, is there a priest aboard, or a holy man?"

"Probably," his dad replied.

"Can I be of some assistance?" Chappy was tapping on Cid's shoulder.

"Chappy, where? How?"

"I found myself in that building over there, standing in front of a large moose head. Hmm, I was in a ticket office at a train station, and then I saw you talking to these people. So, I came over."

"It's my mom and dad and my two baby brothers."

"I know, Cid, and I'm a priest, and I can baptize them for you."

"You would? Thanks."

"Oh, a baptism! Can we be the godparents?"

"What!?"

There stood Columbina, looking her statuesque best, as radiant and beautiful as ever. "They are such beautiful bambinos. I would love to stand for them."

Cid's mom giggled at the bambino reference. "Thank you."

"Oh, and this is Mr. Brecourt. He will be the godfather."

"I would be honored. As much as I would love to give a great speech on this occasion, I will simply say yes."

Chappy then blessed and baptized the two babies.

"Thanks, Cid."

"Dad, I really miss you." Cid then turned to his mum. "I love you, Mum. I'm sorry for making you worry so much, but I turned out fine. I just miss you."

She gave him a big smile, and a tear ran down her cheek. "Thank you, Cid. We both love you, and even more now that the boys are free to join us."

"I love you, Mom, and you too, Dad. I miss you both."

"We're proud of you, Cid, and will always love you."

With that, the train whistled, a conductor yelled, "All aboard!" and the train backed up and left the station.

Cid just stood there amazed and cried. And then he turned around, and Chappy and the two actors were gone. He was smiling and pleased, thankful for the help.

He walked back. Then he thought about it: his brothers, whom he never knew, faced the threat of spending eternity in Limbo because they had no names. At Cid's birth, his mum had been woken from a drug-induced sleep in order to give Cid a name. No one had expected Cid to live. He had been named, baptized, and given his last rites all at once. Then Cid, in a show of obstinance, had lived. He'd spent a few years in the hospital and had recurring nightmares and hallucinations throughout his childhood, but somehow managed to survive. If he'd had no name, he couldn't have been baptized, and if he'd not been baptized, he would be sent to Limbo for eternity.

His brothers had not been given names. Now, they had names. His father had kept two white crosses in their basement that always reminded his family of those two lost to a dreadful fate. Limbo was a terrifying concept that had always haunted Cid. Now, his brothers were free, the curse lifted.

Cid now realized the purpose of Scar's mission, and he agreed with it. These actors needed to be freed from this curse.

He walked right back onto the mountain. He found himself staring at the pirates, who by now were totally confused.

Lusic saw the kid standing in the mist, standing out on what should have been a giant hole. This was the Great Abyss, and here in front of him was one of Scar's friends.

"It's a trick! All of this, it's just some stupid theater trick," Lusic protested.

Gratso shrugged his shoulders and scratched his face. "I don't know, boss. It seems dicey and kind of weird."

Lusic turned to him. "I say it's a trick. He was always doing this kind of thing and escaping, down either some trapdoor or ropes and pulleys. He's set us up. He's not going to get away with it this time."

"I'm with you, boss. Let's go out there and shake them up." Gritso was anxious to do some damage and slammed his fist into his other palm.

"OK, boys, we're going to go get these clowns and finish all this business. I don't care what you do with the others, but leave Scar to me. I'm going in there."

With that, Lusic walked out toward Cid. The rest of his crew followed him as the mist swirled around them.

"You. I know you," Lusic said. "When I'm done with those others, I am coming back here, and you and I are going to have a nice long talk. I remember you. It was outside that theater, wasn't it? Gritso has a bone to pick with you, and I'm going to let him do it."

Cid just stared at him, a mix of emotions swirling in his mind. Then he suddenly felt calm and was no longer afraid. "I'll be waiting, right over there."

So, Cid walked past the pirates, and they just stared and glared and huffed and puffed and then turned and attacked the void. Cid walked over to the rim and sat watching the pirates charge into the Abyss. In a moment, they were gone.

Cid found some wine, poured himself a glass, smelled it, sipped it, and smiled. "Toscana, how nice. How do actors stuck in Limbo obtain Toscana? Actors, I guess, do have their means."

Slowly, the other actors and crew members started to appear, and each had a huge grin on their face and a profound look in their eyes.

Bill and Stan walked out laughing and mock-wrestling with each other. "We've both learned to play the guitar, Cid," Bill announced.

"It's true," said Stan. "We got the chance and took it up, and now, both of us can play. I'm just amazed at how long it took. We must have been in there for years."

"Hello, Cid. Good to see you." Smiley came up and gave Cid a big hug. "Missed you, lad, but I can tell you I've had a few of my prayers answered."

Soon, almost everyone had returned, all with partial answers and satisfactory summarizations of their time in the Abyss.

After a bit, Scar emerged. He walked out of the mist and had everyone gather around.

"Thank you all for trusting me. I've had some of my deepest questions answered thanks to the Great Abyss. My curse, however, cannot be lifted at this moment. I have one more task to accomplish. I need to find holy ground for my crew and Moliere's."

"I know a place." Cid smiled and nodded. "Yes, I know a place. It's where I studied commedia dell'arte. We can sail there and even do a performance at their festival. We will be a surprise. We can do a full commedia. There is a place there, a small burial ground where my teacher is buried. I am sure that he would love the company. We can sail there, and then we can sail back home and return the sailors and fishermen to safe harbors."

Scar grinned. "I like it."

Fred stood up at this moment. "Where's the young boy Dan?"

"Oh, he won't be joining us right now. He's all right. He is just off doing something that he has always loved to do. He's joined the crew of the *Bluenose* and is off fishing on the Grand Banks."

At that point, Brecourt pointed into the mist. "We seem to have invited a pirate to our party."

A solitary garishly dressed pirate came out of the mist. He was talking out loud and pointing at everything he could see. "It is wonderful, so many flowers and so much fun. Oh, look at that cloud. It's beautiful. Do you see it? This is wonderful, oh so wonderful."

Brecourt smiled at him. "Yes, it is wonderful."

"Marvelous," the pirate bellowed. "I am free. I no longer have to kill and maim and scare people. I am free. Oh, look at how green the grass looks."

Smiley looked at the pirate. "I think he was the helmsman from the black ship."

"Black no longer!" the pirate yelled. "It's all colorful, and it will no longer be used to terrify. I am going to sail it somewhere where children can come aboard and laugh and play and enjoy their time on it." With that, he went skipping down the mountain.

Everyone looked at each other, confused and amazed.

CHAPTER 21 EARLIER

L USIC AND HIS MEN WERE READY TO POUNCE. THEY RAN INTO THE swirling mist, waving their sabers. They searched everywhere, and after a while, confusion seeped in. No one was there.

"How did we miss them?" Standing there scratching his chin, staring into the dense fog, Lusic screamed in frustration.

Tiberio suddenly appeared out of the fog. He just walked up to Lusic and bowed. "You wanted me, and here I am. Before you say anything, I wish to say that I am sorry."

Lusic stared at him. "I have waited so long, and all you can say is that you are sorry!"

"It's the best that I could come up with."

"Sorry! I have pursued you for centuries. I have been dreaming about revenge for so long that it has consumed me."

"Well, really, you should just let it go. That's a long time to hold a grudge. Just to let you know, however, it hasn't been easy for me either. I mean, all this time, I have appeared as a goblin. Try doing that for four centuries and a bit. It's not easy. I can't even go into a restaurant."

"I will never let it go!"

"Too bad. I'm sorry to hear that. Well, it's been nice chatting, and oh yes, before I go, I would suggest you not look down." With that, Tiberio disappeared.

Lusic just stared and then shook himself. "Where did he go?" He turned to look at his men, who were all staring at their feet.

Gratso had turned a shade whiter than his usual shady white color. "Boss, I don't like this." He looked up at Lusic and then disappeared downward, screaming all the way. The rest of the pirates soon joined him.

Lusic stepped gingerly backward and then felt nothing as backward he abruptly fell. The pirates fell and fell and fell and eventually faded away. Lusic kept falling.

CHAPTER 22

Dan, after stepping into the fog, found himself on a harbor. There was a sailboat preparing to set sail. He stared at the sailboat; it was a schooner, actually. He rubbed his eyes. It was the *Bluenose*.

Suddenly, a voice called out to Dan. "We're waiting for you, lad. You've signed on as a crew member. Now get yourself aboard, and we'll get moving."

"Yes, sir. I mean, aye, Captain."

"None of that malarkey. Just get up here, go below and stow your belongings, and start learning the ropes. Glad to have you aboard, son."

With that, Dan found himself aboard the real *Bluenose* sailing with his hero, Angus Mcfee.

CHAPTER 23

SCAR NOW FACED THE TWO CREWS OF THE TWO SHIPS.
"My real name is Tiberio Fiorilli. I am asking you all to come with me on one more voyage. We will sail to where Cid has a place, where we can perform and then hold our little ceremony. Chappy here has agreed to bless the place we are going to. It will be sacred ground. So let us all go down this mountain and sail to California. I know that when we do this, my curse will be lifted. I met the person who cursed me and asked for her forgiveness. She said after I achieve this one last task …"

Smiley nudged Cid. "Should we tell him?"

Cid found himself puzzled. "Maybe not. Maybe he doesn't know."

"He's no longer a goblin. We gotta tell him."

Cid quietly mumbled to Smiley. "For now, just go along with it. Maybe he needs to think that he's still cursed."

When they all hiked back down to where their two ships were docked, they could see the pirate ship jauntily sailing away. It looked far more colorful than it had the last time they'd seen it. At the helm was a wildly dressed pirate singing happy songs at the top of his voice.

That night, the two ships' crews stayed at the dock and celebrated their trip up the mountain. No one revealed to Scar that he no longer looked like a goblin, for they didn't know how to begin the conversation. He was convinced that he still looked like a goblin, even when presented with a mirror. In his eyes, he looked like a goblin.

The next day, the two ships set sail for California. The trip up the coast was far more relaxing and quieter than their previous few weeks.

They sailed up the coast until they came to the Mad River. Here, they anchored and the two crews conferred.

Scar stood before the two crews and announced, "We need to go inland here, and the *Bluenose* cannot make this passage, so I need a small crew to stay on board and watch over her. The *Forlorn Hope* is a theater boat, and it has a magic of its own. It will sail up the Mad River, which, in many respects, is impossible. But the *Forlorn Hope* will do it, and it will take the acting troupe with it. It will also take myself, Cid, and Chappy. We need Chappy for this final act. Chappy, Cid, and myself will return to the *Bluenose* after two days. So tonight, let's all say our goodbyes, and tomorrow, we will separate."

The next morning, Cid found himself aboard the *Forlorn Hope* as it sailed up the Mad River. This inland trip's virtual impossibility due to the shallowness of the water caused a bit of concern for many residents. They could not believe what they were seeing, and the mental confusion caused the bulk of those observing to raise no alarm. Truthfully, some questions were raised, but it was too farfetched an idea to believe.

Upon arriving at Blue Lake, the ship quickly transformed itself into a movable stage and arrived next to Odd Fellows Hall. And somehow, posters advertising tonight's show had been plastered all over town and the neighboring towns. An authentic Italian–French commedia troupe would perform tonight during the Dell'Arte Festival of Clowns.

The show was a hit, the crowds ecstatic, and the actors delighted to have an audience. The highlight for Cid was when Tiberio glanced in the mirror before the performance and witnessed that he no longer looked like Scar but saw himself reflected there.

The troupe did two shows that evening; one was Moliere's *The Misanthrope*, and the other was an improv featuring Scaramouche. Scaramouche delighted everyone with his incredible leaps and hilarious facial gestures.

Later that evening, the troupe followed Cid to a quiet little graveyard on the edge of town. Here, Cid led them to the grave where his teacher was buried. "His name was Carlo Mazzone Clementi, and he was my teacher," Cid began. "He was a great man and a wonderful teacher. He founded this school, and I was in his first class. I think he would be honored to have all of you sharing this sacred ground."

With that, Chappy took out his vial of holy water and blessed a spot of earth. He quietly said some lovely words and said a prayer for all of them in Latin. "I hereby bless this spot as holy ground befitting the needs and satisfying the desires of these blessed subjects and lovers of all things holy. Lord, welcome home these dear friends of ours, who are truly creative Christians who have stayed true to their belief in you."

Then they all looked at one another with a mixture of tears, laughter, hugs, kisses, bows, and more tears. Moliere's troupe and Tiberio's company passed into the earth and disappeared.

"We will see you again, Tiberio." Columbina gave her regal wave as she faded away

The three remaining men just stood there for a very long time feeling revered and subdued. Then they turned and walked back to the *Forlorn Hope*. The *Forlorn Hope* now transformed itself into a carriage and took off with them aboard and headed for the river.

"I did it!" was all Tiberio could say.

Upon reaching the river, the *Forlorn Hope* once again became a ship and traveled toward the *Bluenose*.

Once again, the local police were bombarded with phone calls from people who were seeing a ship sailing down the Mad River. None of the reports were documented, however.

Back at the *Bluenose*, the crew watched as the *Forlorn Hope* returned. Scar, Cid, and Chappy soon came back on board the *Bluenose Two*. The *Forlorn Hope* then started to glow and suddenly lifted off the water and sailed up into the heavens, heading east toward the sun.

"I think it's carrying their spirits home." Cid smiled thinking of the actors.

The next day found the *Bluenose* sailing south, beginning its journey back to the Grand Banks. Cid now obtained a journal and began earnestly writing names and making notes and sketches in his book.

CHAPTER 24

WEEKS LATER, RUMORS WERE SPREADING ABOUT SIGHTINGS OF THE *Bluenose Two*. It had been seen off of Argentina. Then a plane had spotted it off Brazil. This news captured the headlines.

The Canadian government sent a frigate to try to capture the wayward ship. Somehow, the fast-moving schooner avoided any capture. The news continued to spread, and in the United States, various sailing schooners began preparing for a race. "Who will catch the *Bluenose*?" became the cry. The schooners started to gather around Miami for what was to be the new America's Cup challenge. Rich, eager challengers prepared for the race. Who would win?

The *Bluenose*, the original one, had been the fastest schooner in its day, having never lost a race, and yet had still been a working fishing schooner. In an office dedicated to The Americas Cup a decision was made to meet the *Bluenose Two* off of Long Island and chase it to Lunenburg. The Racing World had come to life with the news. Sailors with racing crews and sleek ships were eager to pounce. The ship that first passed the *Bluenose Two* would be the top challenger, and the one to beat it to Lunenburg would be the ultimate winner.

So with helicopters circling and yachts of all sizes blaring their horns, the *Bluenose Two* swept past Long Island. The race was on.

Back in Canada, especially Lunenburg, excitement over the race was electric. Canada's pride and joy was returning. They all hoped so, anyway.

Crowds began gathering on the hills along the shore. People from all across Canada were glued to their television sets, awaiting the return. Even the Prime minister and family gathered on the hillside overlooking the waters leading into Lunenburg. The broadcast networks had everything covered. And then one bright morning at about ten o'clock, the crowds of people saw her. A great roar went up, and people were shouting, for there she was, sailing at full sail and being chased by ten or so fast schooners.

Spontaneously, as if on cue, many started singing Stan Rogers's song of the *Bluenose*. A recording of Stan singing was being broadcast on speakers from a stage set up on one of the hills. When Stan belted out the words "That's the *Bluenose*," everyone wept and cheered and then went on singing.

It looked as if a shadow appeared out at sea beyond the *Bluenose Two*, and that was when the miracle of the *Bluenose* happened. There sailing beside the *Bluenose Two* was another schooner, its twin. People on the shore screamed and cried and hugged each other. Some fell to their knees.

The chasing ships floundered and lost the wind in their sails. On the open ocean a few miles from Lunenburg, the *Bluenose Two* was being accompanied by the *Bluenose*. Mother and daughter sailed majestically together and then promptly disappeared.

It had all been caught on camera, so no one could deny it. It sent shock waves through the nation. No one could explain it. The Canadian mint then started minting twenty-cent pieces with the two boats on it. Meanwhile, *Little Bluey* still sat in Lunenburg Harbor guarded by the RCMP.

Sometime later, two sailing ships approached the Grand Banks. For a brief moment, the two ships were anchored side by side, and Dan managed to board the *Bluenose Two*. Angus waved him off, and the *Bluenose* sailed away.

Dan stood on deck. "I've had the time of my life," he said. He just stood there, grinning and looking around the deck.

"Good to have you back, Dan." Tiberio approached him. "It's me, Scar. I've been changed back to my right looks."

"It's an improvement, I must say," responded Dan.

The sailors all came over and clapped Dan on the back. Tubbs stood back and looked him up and down. "Looks like you grew out a bit, Dan—gained some muscle there."

"Was that old Angus you were sailing with?" Fred interjected.

"Yes, it was."

"You are a lucky lad. Many a Maritimer would give anything for that experience." He stood there shaking his head.

"Lucky is right. It was hard work but very satisfying. He is, was … whatever. I have a lot of respect for him."

Bill and Stan stood before Dan. Bill reached out and shook Dan's hand. "I bet you know every knot now."

"I learned them real well; I had to know them, or else. That's what he said to me, but I never figured out what 'or else' was. I learned them all right."

"Good," Stan chimed in, "but we still get some credit for teaching you."

"Absolutely!"

"I'm glad to see you. I was a bit worried that we had lost you." Cid let out a sigh and gave Dan a hug. "Well, I guess now we have to get everyone back to their homes and their own time zones." Cid said this out loud, but in truth, he had no idea how Tiberio was going to do this.

"Remember what I originally said to you, Cid?"

Cid stared at Tiberio for a while. Then it dawned on him. "Theater magic!"

"That's right." Tiberio stood there grinning with his arms folded over his chest. The grin reminded Cid of Tiberio's goblin look.

"OK, you got me," gasped Cid. "Just tell me so I don't go batty."

"We have to wait for the curtain call. You know, wait for the cue."

Cid just stood there with mouth open. The rest of the crew looked equally confused.

"The fog is the cue. We wait here for the fog, and then everyone climbs back into their dories and returns to their home schooners. Before you all get frightened, they will be there. When you hear a ship's bell, follow it. As to you five sailors, your life raft will be here, and as soon as you get in it, a rescue ship will find you—all except you, Chappy. I need you to come with me. It's your choice, however. But I will get you home and in your time. You can meet up with your shipmates sometime later."

Chappy looked perplexed. "These are my shipmates. I can't just abandon them."

"It's temporary. I'll have you back in Britain just when they arrive."

"Promise?"

"Yes, I promise. You are going to be saved by a little fishing boat that will take you back to a safe harbor. Then I need you to come with me and bless one more spot. It's where I was buried."

"What?" Both Chappy and Cid were startled and blurted out the same question.

"They believed that I was dead. I wasn't in the coffin. It was a dummy. It's complicated. I just need you to do this, please."

Chappy agreed and then turned to his shipmates. "I trust him, boys, and look what he did for those actors. We will meet in Britain somewhere and give thanks for surviving."

At that point, Reggie came over and stood before Tiberio. "What's to keep us from telling anybody about what we have been through, Tiberio?"

"Actually, that doesn't bother me," Tiberio said. "Do you think anybody will really believe you?"

Reggie's face looked odd, part scowl and part bewilderment. Then he relaxed and just laughed. "No, I guess not. It would be a mouthful of a yarn, however."

"Feel free, Reggie. Your grandkids will love to hear your tall tales. I say let's have a little feast and then say our goodbyes."

After a resounding shout of ayes, they all commenced rounding up some food and any musical instrument they could find and spent the afternoon celebrating their voyage.

Late in the afternoon, a fog came in. Everyone grew quiet.

"It's time, boys. Let's see each other off." Tiberio walked around shaking each and every crew member's hand.

Cid stood with Darcy. "I told you he would get you home."

"You did, and I'm grateful. I'll never see you again, Cid. Not ever."

"I know, but then, I'll never forget you."

With that, they hugged, and try as they might, they couldn't help but shed a tear.

"You go find your dad and go home and raise a family. Take care, Darcy."

"Thanks. Write some books. And maybe you should go and meet some girl."

"I'll do that. It's a plan."

Darcy went over the side and got into his dory. Surprisingly, it was filled with fish. He pushed off. Then he turned his head as if he'd heard something. He turned back and waved and then rowed toward the sound he had heard.

The twins had the same experience. Bill was excitingly pointing toward the west, and both he and Stan rowed their dories in that direction.

After a while, all the fisherman were gone. Tiberio turned to the four sailors. "Your turn, men."

Stefan shook Tiberio's hands. "Thank you. It's been strange and it's been an adventure, and it saved us from this awful war for a short while."

"You will be fine, Stefan. I know that you will make it home safely."

"How?"

"I can't answer that, but while in the Abyss, I got some reassurance. I am just trusting in that."

Tubbs shot his arm in. "Well, I'm glad you are not a goblin, although you were all right as a goblin."

"Thanks, Tubbs. It's been a pleasure. Good shooting, by the way, with those paint cannons."

Tom interjected, "Hey, we're professionals."

"I'll see you guys off, and I'll take Chappy safely home also," Tiberio told them.

The men then all turned on Chappy, hugged and slapped him, and climbed overboard, calling out, "Cheerio!" and "Tata!" and "Won't be long." As they settled into the raft, however, apprehension could be seen on their faces.

"I'll say a prayer for you boys, and when we get together again, let's have a sacred beer." With that, Chappy lifted their spirits, and they appeared to relax.

Soon, the fog enveloped their life raft, and they disappeared from view. On the raft, Stefan looked at the other three. "I guess we have to just trust that it all—"

Tubbs cut him off. "Look!" He was pointing to the east. There, coming out of the mist, which was now clearing, was a frigate—a Royal Canadian frigate. "God, we're saved!"

Fred piped in. "Tiberio was as good as his word."

Stefan, with a grin on his face, replied, "He sure was!"

As the frigate stopped beside them, from up above came a voice. "You fellas need a ride?"

Tiberio, Cid, Dan, and Chappy now stood alone on the *Bluenose Two.*

"What was all that about theater magic, Tiberio?" Chappy asked him.

"It's a bit, well, it's how we got this here boat. However, once we stop using it, Dan here will go home. I'm sure you would like to go home, Dan."

Dan responded, "Of course I would, but I can't say that I haven't enjoyed this. It's been the time of my life. It actually has been magical. We really did save those folks who were stuck in Limbo."

"Yes, we did. They were my friends, and I couldn't have done it without you. Now, when we do this, you are going to be back in Lunenburg on this schooner. We will be on another boat. It's a boat really close to Cid's heart. I see you smiling, Cid. Dan, as Cid starts to see his boat, this one will disappear, and you and the *Bluenose* will leave us. Thank you, Dan."

They all shook hands, and slowly, the *Bluenose* and Dan disappeared, and Cid, Tiberio, and Chappy found themselves at sea on the *Little Bluenose.*

"Let's head back to Scotland." Tiberio said.

In Lunenburg, a bewildered RCMP officer screamed in shock as the *Bluenose Two* suddenly reappeared, moored to the dock. "This is the second time this schooner has made me drop my coffee!"

Dan, standing at the helm, just smiled at him.

Soon, reporters were scrambling, and officers were trying to nab him. A real hullabaloo was taking place on the pier at Lunenburg.

At first, Chappy was in a state of shock over the change of ship. He walked around the little fishing boat, handling and touching everything.

"Theater magic," he kept saying. It took him awhile to get over it. Cid and Tiberio just handled the little ship, sailing it eastward.

The *Little Bluenose* sailed admirably; Cid now looked like a veteran as he managed the little fishing boat. The three of them shared the sailing duties and much conversation as they headed home. Tiberio's plan was to sail right back to where they had started. The only difference was that Cid would arrive a few months after he left and Chappy and Tiberio would arrive in 1943. How Tiberio was managing all of this, Cid could only guess. Actually, he couldn't figure it out at all and just went along with it.

"I have to see that Chappy gets home safely," Tiberio pointed out and then shrugged. "I also need him to come with me to do for me what he did for my friends. Then he has to see that the right person gets this little ship so that you can eventually buy it."

"You knew that I would buy it?"

"Of course. As you can see, I helped write the script. Chappy is also going to buy your little house, and eventually, you will discover it and buy it also—not that I am manipulating anything. I'm just smoothing things out." With that Tiberio grinned.

"Thanks,' said Cid looking out at the horizon. "Will I ever see you again?"

"I don't know, because I can't see beyond when we separate. It's all new to me after that. I suspect that I will depart this world at some time, but I'm not sure when." Tiberio just shrugged and patted Cid on the shoulder.

Chappy had been listening to all of this and just quietly nodded. He then made a *hmm* sound and spoke. "It's been an odd adventure, this. Tiberio, I suspect that you would like to see things wrapped up and make your curtain call. The timing is not my say or influence, but I am glad to help you in any way I can. Cid, this has been a great experience, and I cherish your friendship." With that, he shook Cid's hand and hugged him. "Take care of yourself, and God be with you."

"Thank you, Chappy." Cid found himself with tears in his eyes.

At that point, Tiberio looked at Cid and also gave him a big hug. "It's time, Cid. We are going to leave you here. I can see the lighthouse near your home."

"Now!" Cid stared at the horizon, and there it was. He turned to say something to Tiberio and realized that both Tiberio and Chappy were fading away.

"I don't like long goodbyes, so take care, Cid. Write those books and give those characters names. That way, you can sleep at night. Oh, and say hello to that girl you are going to meet."

"What?" Cid stared at the two as they faded and disappeared.

There was still a ship to steer, and this took up Cid's attention as his house and dock came into view.

As Cid sailed into his little harbor and neared the pier that awaited him, he saw a woman with long brown hair standing on the pier. She waved.

"Hello. Welcome home. Toss me a line; I'll help you moor. I'm Ellen, by the way."

"Ellen?"

"Yes, I wrote you about buying your little boat."

They both set about mooring the boat to the dock.

"Don't sell it," she told him. "It would be a shame to sell such a dear little boat."

"OK. Would you like to come up to the house for tea?"

"I'd love to."

With that, the two of them headed up to the house.

Cid, by the way, was smitten.

EXPLANATIONS

I N A SENSE, THIS STORY IS A BIT OF AN IMPROVISATION. I TRIED TO formulate it using different approaches to writing but finally gave up and allowed myself to improvise. In other words, I shut up and just wrote it.

Moliere did, in fact, exist and is known as France's Shakespeare. His plays are wonderfully written and quite funny. Moliere's acting troupe was popular with the king of France and shared a theater with a commedia dell'arte troupe led by Tiberio Fiorilli. The companies performed on alternate nights.

Tiberio is famous for creating a character called Scaramouche, which is what the French knew him as. It is said that Moliere would stand backstage and with a mirror try to recreate Scaramouche's facial acrobatics.

Commedia troupes started in Italy and were basically improv troupes. Characters were created from the stock characters of the different regions of Italy, and actors would play their characters for their whole careers. Generally, the actors wore half masks that symbolized, or more likely represented, these characters. Scaramouche, however, wore white face; his own face was his mask. Moliere's comedies borrowed from these stock characters, and the commedia melded into his work.

Moliere died suddenly. He was well loved. Actors, however, were not thought highly of, and he made enemies. Moliere seemed to make the aristocracy, including the Church, targets of farce.

France was a Catholic country at this time. Upon Moliere's death, the local Bishop of the Church declared that Moliere could not be buried in hallowed ground. This is a terrible concept for Catholics because it means they cannot go to heaven. One version of the story I have heard says that the king went to the pope to beg permission on bended knee, and another says that he went to a cardinal. I embellished it; I like the pope version. At any rate, Moliere's burial in hallowed ground was allowed, but only on one condition: none of his actors could ever be buried in hallowed ground. Thus, they were doomed.

This story has personal meaning to me, as I was born Roman Catholic. At my birth, it was thought that I would not survive. As a result, my mother had to name me so that I could be baptized and given my last rites. I fooled everyone, however, and lived. Two of my brothers were not so lucky, and the idea of them being in Limbo concerned me. I do not wish to be morose. I feel that I have freed them and they have inspired my creativity. Thank you, bros.

I studied commedia dell'arte with a man named Carlo Mazzone Clementi at his school in Northern California. I was one of his first students. I have often described the experience as "Carlo would take you to the edge of the Abyss, and then he would teach you dance." I loved Carlo and am eternally grateful to him.

Being Canadian, I also have carried around and looked at our little dime forever, and I love the story of the *Bluenose*. If you don't know the story, please research it.

Everything in this story is fictional. I just wanted to uplift people, and I had fun being creative. If you read this book, thank you.

Ingram Content Group UK Ltd.
Milton Keynes UK
UKHW020711210423
420559UK00015B/921